UNLIMITED *Faith*

WHEN YOU THINK YOUR FAITH HAS RUN OUT

SHAKEEMA S. PERRY

ISBN: 9798715410986

DEDICATION

I dedicate this book to my Lord and Savior Jesus Christ because He is my everything, and He is the inspiration of this book. God is my Rock & Foundation; I shall not be moved. Thank you, Lord, for being my Coach; you have coached me into my destiny, and I am very grateful, and I owe you everything. I will continue to obey because obedience is better than sacrifice, and that is all I know since I have given my heart to you in my mid 20's. I am about to be 40 yrs old, and I still have the same or even more tenacity to serve you.

You have been with me through my roughest moments, and I would not be able to survive without your love and grace and your pure kindness. You love your people. That is why you inspired me to write this book because faith is the essence of who you are and what you do and what you expect all of us to do. Is to believe that anything is possible through you. I love you and I pray that you keep on using me for Your glory, because you deserve all of it, and I will continue to make you PROUD!!!

From Your Daughter,
Shakeema S. Perry

CONTENTS

INTRODUCTION

This book was created for all believers in Jesus Christ and non-believers, because after you read this book, trust me that will change. I know that some of us want to believe in the big bang theory that this earth was created like it just happened. But we all know deep down that, this theory is far from the truth.

For example, if the earth was created with a big bang, how come the creation is so detailed, how come our mouth, eyes, and teeth are structured? That could not happen with a big bang, neither can any other source have come up with this beautiful earth created. Only God Himself could create something so amazing and detailed the way it is. God is a God that created Himself and the earth. He commanded the earth to come to existence with His voice.

Genesis Chapter 1:1-3 says, "*In the beginning God created [by forming from nothing] the heavens and the earth. The earth was formless and void or a waste and emptiness, and darkness was upon the face of the deep [primeval ocean that covered the unformed earth]. The Spirit of God was moving (hovering, brooding) over the face of the waters. And God said, Let their be light*"; and there was light."

You see, according to these scriptures, God commanded this world into existence, it just was not created on its own. When God created man, He intended for us to have that same power as He did and still does. That is why we were created in His image and His likeness. The problem with man is that some of us lost that power because of the lack of belief in God and ourselves.

The relationship with God diminished and we exclude ourselves from the instructions given to us by our creator. God's true intentions for us is for us to have dominion over the earth, but we lack the belief that we have dominion. The reason that we lack that powerful insight is that we turned away from God and what He purposed for us to accomplish on earth.

We all have an assignment on this earth that God is expecting us to fulfill, but we don't know what that is, because we fail to seek God for the answers concerning our purpose in life. God never gave us the promise that it was going to be easy. But He did give us the promise that He will be with you every step of the way. So, if you think that fulfilling purpose is easy, you will be sadly mistaken. Because with purpose there is always a process. But it is a good process because it forms you into being more like Christ. Confident, Resilient, Full of Faith, Patient all of the fruits of the Spirit.

When we allow God to take us through this faith process, we will win in the end. But we have to let God guide us through this path called life so we can get to where He wants us to be. Remember this faith that you have or will have is not only for you; it is also for someone else to believe God's promises and believe Him for their path to success in life. This book is called Unlimited Faith because God has given to us, we just have to believe we have it.

Chapter 1

Premature Faith

Faith is a journey that never ends in your life. It will always be part of every step you take. Faith is not always used for good; it depends on what you believe in. You can believe the in wrong thing; it is still considered faith. But it will take you down the path of destruction. When you believe the right kind of faith, it will take you to places that you have never imagined.

Growing up, I believed in God, but I became a Christian when I was 11 years old. I did not know exactly what it was all about, but my parents trained me to go to church, so that was all I knew. I knew about God, but I did not know Him in a personal way. I did not have a relationship with Him. I only talked to God when I was in need of something.

That was not a true relationship that I had with Him. So when situations began to happen, distractions here and there, I fell apart because I had no root of faith in me to sustain me in my tough times. In essence, faith is critical to a believer. It is pretty much our lifeline, not physically but spiritually. Also, it is important to a non-believer, believe it or not. Faith does not only work for the believer it also works for a non-believer.

The difference is that the believer believes in God by faith that He will come through any opposition that he or she is going through. A non-believer believes only in themselves that they will make it through their opposition. But the only thing the non-believer is limited, because we have limitations as humans. But I can say sometimes the non-believer is more successful than the believer. Why is that?

It should be the opposite right? We have a supernatural power that others don't have. We should be progressing on a greater level than anyone in this world who do not have this type of power. The problem is with some of us Christians, OH NO, don't close the book. Listen to this truth. There are some Christians that say they believe in God, but do not put their faith into action. Faith is an action word.

You cannot say that you have faith without taking action on what you are believing God for. Faith is not a noun; it is a verb, the meaning of faith is complete trust or confidence in someone or something. Another meaning is that faith requires an action of some sort, that act is supposed to be precipitated by the understanding what you do based upon what you believe.

Faith cannot stand alone it needs a friend and that friend is called action. How can you believe something so strongly and do not act on it. That is not real faith, if you think that is faith, then you have been misled what faith really is. The Bible says:

"By faith Abel offered unto God a more excellent sacrifice," (Hebrews 11:4)

"By faith Abraham when he was called to go [by God], obeyed by going to a place which he was to receive as an inheritance; and he

9

went not knowing where he was going." (Hebrews 11:8)

That is how faith works, it is unknown to you but known to God. Under the basics of faith, there are 5 kinds of faith in the Bible. The first kind of faith is saving faith. This is the believer's initial faith, this happens when you first get saved and confess Jesus Christ as your Lord and Savior. It is the faith that God imparts to the believer for salvation. It is a gift as none of us had this faith unless God first bestows it upon us. The Bible says:

For it is by grace [God's remarkable compassion and favor drawing you to Christ] that you have been saved [actually delivered from judgment and given eternal life] through faith, and this [salvation] is not of yourselves [not through your own effort], but it is the [undeserved, gracious] gift of God.

There are more types of faith, but it will be discussed subsequently in this book. Faith cannot be seen; it is an internal belief. It is from the inside out. It requires you to believe in your heart then, it will be followed by action. Through action, you will start to implement faith moves in your life. I like to call it faith mode.

 A mode is a way or manner in which something occurs or is expressed, experienced, or done. I like to do things a certain way. I love to tap into my faith in an unusual way, because that allows me not to give up when opposition comes my way. This book was written by faith. I am already a published author, and after I wrote my first book, I was pushing for sales, and I did pretty good the first six months, then my sales slowed down little to nothing.

So what was I going to do? I kept pushing sales, but I got very discouraged because it was not working like I thought it would. I started to look at other authors and see what they did to be successful. I learned that they kept on going and kept on writing even when their books flopped or did not do well. They kept on coming out with books, and then they started to see their bestselling books start selling and becoming a #1 bestselling author. It was their passion in the writing and that is my passion as well. So what did I do, I started to write this book and will start writing more so I will have a larger plethora of books to sell to my audience.

I want my books not to only impact my life, I want my books to impact the world. When I write, I know someone will be encouraged on what I have to say and start to believe again. Writing also gives me a sense of peace, and it helps me as well to write to you. This book actually demonstrates my life and walk with God. During my journey, I always had to put my faith in the for front of my life. If I had not I would not be able to survive now and what is ahead. Now is the reality, and your faith is what's ahead. So I have to believe no matter the degree of what's happening now.

Chapter 2

Faith Under Pressure

I have to mention this, at this current time, the world is going through a crisis of Covid-19 pandemic. Over 1 million people have died across the globe, and hundreds of thousands in the United States alone. This is our current reality in the world and someone may think while reading this book, 'Wow, you are writing in such a time of crazy and chaotic time that the world is going through the worst pandemic ever.

It's Ironic that you said that and I know it seems so crazy to write a book in all this madness, but I would say to you this is the best time to write. We were on lockdown and stay at home order and also some of us now work from home. This is the perfect time to either write your story or something you were thinking of writing but never got around to it. It is your time and season to write. This pandemic is not forever.

God is using this time to draw His people closer to Him. At a time like this, God wants to have a stronger relationship and also to grab His people's attention to what is going on in our society, and we have to be ready for whatever comes. I believe in this time that people will give their heart to the Lord Jesus Christ more they ever before.

Also just like this book, God is giving us unlimited faith, a faith that has no end. Let's look at the word unlimited. Unlimited means not limited or restricted in terms of numbers, quantity, or extent. That means that your faith can be at a level that will never end, but you have to believe that with all of you.

There are times that you will have doubt, but that is normal. You just cannot stay in doubt. You need to have a growth mindset, believing that you will not always be where you currently are today, but be grateful for not being what you used to be. Every year you should progress on projects or aspects of your life.

A year from now you will be in a better place. As long as you don't lose the principle of faith, which means, you are constantly working toward your dreams and goals. It is through this progress that you manifest the change you want. You have to make a decision in faith that your life must experience a shift, but don't blame anyone else for what you did not do. You have the power to change your story. You don't have to live in your past when you can change your future today.

You need to take the lead in your life and every situation you face by declaring a change by speaking it out of your mouth. You have the responsibility to declare over your life every good thing that you are expecting and see them come to pass. For example, proclaim and say that you are wealthy, even when your bank account is low, you have to believe that is who you are no matter what happens in your life.

The Bible says:

"Who shall ever separate us from the love of Christ? Will tribulation, or distress, or persecution, or famine, or nakedness, or

danger, or sword?" Romans 8:35

This book was inspired on what I believe and who I believe in. I don't take any credit of my belief system, also the victories I have experienced. Also how I overcame life issues on my journey. If you read or have read my first book, "The Mind Regulator" you will understand why I am saying this. It was nothing but God that delivered my mind from torment. It was all God and faith moves that I had to take in order to survive that tough time I was in. If I did not walk in true faith; believing and taking action in my situation, I would never be where I am today.

I am an entrepreneur, author, homeowner and the list goes on and on. There are so many things that God had done and the list is endless. It definitely took my faith and works to get there. Was it easy? Absolutely no. Was it worth it, I am screaming Yes! to the top of my lungs. My story was already written by God, I just had to believe Him for the middle, He already knew where I would end up.

He also wrote and know your story, but you must follow Him in order to see the victory in your life. You have to believe Him for the in-between. I know it can be or get really rocky, and you start to believe the lie of the enemy. The devil would tell you nothing will work out for you but that is a lie. Know that God had already set up the blueprint for your life. You just have to believe it and except it. Then faith can take root in you and you can survive anything that comes your way. So don't be so quick to believe the total opposite of what God already said that you have. The Bible says:

"So faith comes from hearing [what is told], and what is heard comes by the [preaching of the] message concerning

Christz." Romans 10:17

This will have you faith on 100, when you study and read the word of God out loud. When you hear the word of God in your ears, it does something on the inside of you that I cannot explain. It brings a confidence in you, even when you have nothing to show for it. No evidence, it is just the assurance in God's word. I love reading the word of God, especially the stories on how God brought His people through.

One of my favorites is Joseph and how his brothers did him so dirty by faking his death and selling him off to slavery. Then years went by, and for the first time that they saw Joseph again, they did not recognize him. Joseph did know that it was his brothers and he remembered what they did. What his brothers did not realize was that God used the evil they did to Joseph for his good. It taught Joseph how to walk by faith in God and have a stronger relationship with Him.

His journey was necessary for his growth, or he would not have been able to rule when the famine came to the land. This was also fulfilling prophesy that God had revealed to Joseph when he had a dream that his family would bow down to him. It was all part of God's major plan for his life. It did not look good at the beginning but his end was blessed. Joseph truly had faith because that prophesy took 17 years before it happened. I love what the number 17 means. It means complete victory overcoming the enemy. What was meant for evil in Joseph's life turned around for his good.

Faith takes a lot of patience; it is not automatic. When you move by faith, it does not mean everything you believe in will be yours as soon as possible. The Bible says:

"Be assured that the testing of your faith [through experience] produces endurance [leading to spiritual maturity, and inner peace]." James 1:3

So your faith is tried by fire. It builds stamina, confidence, and maturity in God as you wait on God after you did your part and moved by faith. It is not easy to wait, but waiting is good for us, because when we get there we will appreciate it the more. It won't be treated like junk, it will be treated as treasure. When I got my house it was not an easy process. I almost did not get it, but God eventually blessed me with it. I treated it like gold, I really did appreciated it more than I would have done if it came so easy. These things that I experience catapulted my faith to another level.

My faith was on a greater level, the reason I can say that now is because of what I have been through and how God brought me out. Earlier I said that growing up, I did not know God, because I never built a relationship with him. But now I am 15 years strong with my relationship with God, that I have enough experience to know that He would see me through anything that I faced and will ever face in my life. I can say that with full confidence. Don't get me wrong, I do have my days of doubt, but I do not stay there very long. All I have to do is, look at God and all the wonderful things He has done and remember what He told me about my future already. This will put my mind back on track.

Or maybe you will say that you don't have that experience with God yet. Look at the simple things in life, like getting up in the morning and having all of your limbs. Maybe you have birth defects, remember that you are here for a reason and a purpose and God can still use you. So never look at your limitations or see it as the reason why God will not do it for you, because you can do something and that something is greater than your limitations. God made you limited for a reason, and that reason is so you can depend on him and He will make you unlimited with his strength and power.

The Bible says that it is impossible to please God without faith. My faith helps me to grow on levels that I have never experienced. I can tell you that so many times when I trusted God, He came through every single time. I am not saying that it happened the way I thought it would happen, but He did it the way it was supposed to happen. It is God's will to bless us, but we just have to receive what God has for us.

 We cannot walk in fear and say that it is faith. Fear is a counterfeit and the opposite of faith. What does faith mean to you? Have you ever ask yourself that question? Think about it and write it down, does it align with what the Bible says or it is something you believed because someone told you that is the definition of faith. You should really think about it so you can have the right mindset of what faith really is in your life.

Faith does not have limitations, it can grow as big as you desire, but you have to exercise your faith. You may ask the question, how do you exercise your faith? You have to start making some faith moves even if you fail, because the more you do it, the more you will start to see victories. When you move by faith on something you are believing God for, you will start to build a track record from God that you can go by anytime you bump into a challenge. Then it will get to a place that you make faith moves without thinking, by that time, your faith would have increased and it will become a part of you. It will feel like it is the normal thing to do now.

Some people will look at you like you are crazy, but you are not. Build up your faith so much that your level of thinking is different from everyone else around you. Not like you are better than them, you just think differently. Now, you can help others get to your level of thinking.

My dad has this level of thinking, which was what I truly started from when it came to my faith. My dad brought a brand new car for $100 and the person that sold it to him was a racist. You may ask the question, how did he do that? First, to give you a backdrop, my dad had a car that was broke down and smoking, and he was tired of my sisters and I laughing when the cops kept on stopping him because it was not safe on the road. My dad was so tired of what he was going through, so by faith, my dad was so determined to get a new car that he was not leaving until he had the keys.

Not in a forceful way, but my dad talked the man into believing that he will have some more money next week for more of a down payment, which my father did not have at the moment. But my dad has been a business owner for over 40 years, but at the time, I would say almost 20 years. But he knew he would get the money and the man believed him.

My dad said that the Holy Spirit, which is God told him what to say to the man to get him to give him the car, because God knew that my dad was a man of faith and he would get that money. My dad was someone that did not talk; he moved by faith in everything he does. Guess what? That car key was released into my dad's hands. My father drove off the lot with my sisters and I in the car, and sure enough, my dad had the money the next week to pay the dealership. That is true faith, I believe when you trust God on that level He is not going to fail you, He will back you up. God doesn't play with faith he honors it.

It does not matter who says no or who you think will say no. God has the final say, so if it is yours, then no one or nothing can hold it back from you. God can change the heart of man, just like He changed a racist heart toward my dad. The word of God says,

"And I will make Pharaoh's heart hard, and multiple my signs and wonders (miracles) in the land of Egypt." Exodus 7:3

The Lord can harden and soften the heart of man for His glory and your benefit. God is so amazing when it comes to the Spirit of faith. If it is His will, He will back you up. Sometimes it is His wisdom that guides you. We as people will not know everything, that is why we go through a process in life. We can't know everything, because we will not learn or grow.

Also in some cases it may not be a no, but it could be a not yet. There are some things we are not ready for, and God holds them back from us until we are ready. So in order to know more of what His will is for your life you will have to spend more time with Him. The more you build a relationship with Him, the more you know how He moves and how He wants you to move.

There are 3 things that I experience with God concerning Him answering my prayers. He will say Yes, No or Not Yet. When He says, yes, move on it right away, don't wait. If He said, no, don't move forward because it is not going to work out, if you do, it will just be a waste of your time. Not yet is tricky because this deals with the timing of God, you have to wait until God says okay or if He brings it to you in your spirit on a later date. You just have to be sensitive to the Holy Spirit to know the difference.

God has a lot of ways he can speak to His children, for us to understand what He is saying. He can speak directly to you, use His word to show you, and he can use a person to give you guidance. There are several ways God can communicate. But it is important to use your discernment, especially when it comes to people. You have to make sure who is speaking in your life hears from God too. You would not go to a dentist for heart surgery. You would have to do the same for your life, be careful who counsels you spiritually.

I would say a good example of a counselor would be your Pastor, Elder of the Church. But someone you know that is mature in Christ. Because all leaders are not mature. That is why you use discernment, meaning, try the spirit by the spirit, ask, does this person bears good fruit? Does He follow God's word?

God also confirm His word either directly or through the word of God, but you will know, so don't be afraid to go for it. When you do, it will show forth in time, sometimes it is not revealed right away.

Chapter 3

Faith is an Action Word

Have you ever hear that faith without works is dead? It is in the word of God in James 2:17. We always have to back our faith with work or action because faith cannot move on its own. It needs help and that help is the action that we take to back up faith after we declared it out of our mouth. Know that faith is waiting, on your next move, so what are you going to do with the faith that God has given you. Are you going to let it go to the grave, or are you going to nurture it and watch it grow to a point that it becomes a part of you.

Faith is something that is in you from God and we all have a measure of it, but we have to cultivate the faith by exercising it daily, in our lives. The more we use it the more it will grow. You may ask how do you use it so it can grow? The first thing is building a relationship with God, by praying, reading God's word, and just walk in what you desire to do by faith.

You may have moments of failure, but you have to get back up and keep going. Don't let anyone or anything stop you. People will try to discount or discourage your faith by speaking negative things against your goals and dreams that you are believing God for. That is why you have to get people that are going to encourage your faith, not damage your faith. The Bible says that your faith can move mountains, not literally, but when you have faith, you move things out of your way that was stopping you from moving forward. For example; I was traveling from Bahamas and I did not know that the plane that I went on was a'la carte which means you pay for everything separately including luggage, drinks etc.

My bag cost $65 to board the plane, which I thought was highway robbery, because I paid the same price going to Bahamas. So I had to wait at the airport for a 2 hour flight delay and I was already upset about the luggage and now our plane was late. So I asked if I can get the bag on the plane for free or at least some type of discount. The flight attendant said no and then I asked can I speak to her supervisor. The supervisor came and she said no too, I was livid at that time.

I said this is nothing but the devil and I spoke this right out of my mouth and said with all this drama something good is about to happen. I was so on it, because I spoke it and tried to do something with action to get my luggage on the plan for free because of the inconvenience of me waiting. We actually had to switch gates because the plane could not land at the current gate we were located. Guess what happened, because we were at a different gate they were new staff and when I was boarding the plane the lady said you can go, but next time you will have to pay.

You see because I took action and also spoke life into my situation God open the door and went over the supervisor's head because she tried to block me from getting something that God wanted me to have and that was to keep the money in my pocket because I spent so much money on this trip. Even the supervisor could not do anything, God is the boss over everyone and He has the final say even when someone tells you no. Your faith can take you anywhere that God is giving you the green light to go. So seize every moment you have because it is very valuable to where you are going. You cannot go far in life without faith, because the opposite of faith is fear.

Fear stops you in your tracks. Fear causes you not to believe anything that you are capable of. It snatches your identity, it steals your life, your time, family etc… If you walk in fear, in your whole life, you will not be able to reach the full potential that God intended for your life. You would not know what was in you all along. You will not know what you are capable of doing and who you are. So fear cannot live in your life. You have to cast it down like the Bible says: We are destroying sophisticated arguments and every exalted and proud thing that sets itself up against the [true] knowledge of God, and we are taking every thought and purpose captive to the obedience of Christ. (2nd Corinthians 10:5)

Your life is in God's hands. Faith in God is the reason that most of us are here today. If it was not for Him, we will not be able to survive the rough times. Prayer is the key and faith unlocks the door. Faith will unlock many doors for you that you cannot see yet. But what faith does is, it allows you to see it before you see it. Did you ever had a vision of something you wanted and then you went to get it and then you had it. That is how faith works; you envision your dream first, then you start making faith steps toward that vision to make it your reality. Faith gives you a vision to where you are going to be.

Life is short. Life is what you make it and you have to make it count. How do you do that? It is by allowing your faith to take over your thoughts and mind so you can believe the impossible even in the hardest time and season of your life. Faith is like the air. You can't see it, but you can feel it on the inside of you telling you to move forward. Even when you feel fear trying to grip you, but faith is holding you up. That is what happens when you continue to exercise your faith. You keep your faith in practice no matter what.

Just like a boxer that wants to win a fight and he practices his skills to make sure he gains victory over his contender. That is just like you, your faith is your skill, when you practice your faith by getting up every day, maximizing your time, by working your business plan, getting knowledge concerning your business, setting up your LLC for your business. That is you practicing your faith skills and that is how you become a pro in putting your faith into action like a boxer. You may not see what's coming down the road, but your faith does.

I was using a business as an example, but it can be anything it could be you opening up that bakery finally, or going after that new promotion at your job or anything that you are passionate about and believing God for.

That is why you continue to push harder no matter how much it hurts or how much work it takes, or how long it takes for you to get there. It took me time to get this book done, but I was not going to quit until I get this book in your hands. That is true faith endurance, because you will get there eventually as long as you still believe that you will. You cannot have a give up-mentality when you are walking in faith, you must have a major mentality when it comes to your faith.

What does that mean? A major mentality is when you think in a major place then where you are currently in order to see yourself where you want to be. It is all in your head; you can either have a defeated mentality or a major mentality. I choose major, how about you? It is definitely your choice, you have to choose what type of life you want to live.

 But faith is waiting for you to grab it, not the other way around. Faith is not going to chase you down; you have to chase it down and never let it go. The second type of faith is called "The Fruit of Faith" The fruit of faith is the one we use to living a Christian lifestyle; this faith is called the faith of righteousness. Romans 1:17. This faith comes by the Holy Spirit living in you and starts to pick up the character of God by faith and take His lifestyle of peace, prosperity, favor, love etc.

This is another type of faith, and it is the most important one, because this faith is required in order to obtain the favor of what God wants to give you in an unlimited way. Also, this type of faith will determine your eternal destiny. You need faith in every area of your life, because that is the only way to walk in the unlimited. It is not only one area in your life, it is all the areas of your life that you have to tap into your faith. Take a few minutes and write down some areas in your life that you fear the most. Then when you are done, declare out of your mouth that the areas that you fear will have no existence in your life. You will now walk in faith in each area you feared before.

For example you fear dogs, then you say I do not fear dogs I have dominion over every creature upon the face of the earth. The Bible says:

"Then God said, let us (Father, Son, Holy Spirit) make man in our image, according to our likeness [not physical, but a spiritual personality and moral likeness]; and let them have complete authority over the fish of the sea, the birds of the air, and over the entire earth, and over everything that creeps and crawls on the earth." Genesis 1:26

We actually have dominion over every animal and insect of the earth. We do not have to be afraid of any of them, because God set it up that way. But if we don't know that, we will entertain fear in all aspects of our lives. That is why it is very important to stay connected to God's word. It stabilizes and takes root in you, so you will be able to discern everything that you hear and you will know, what and what not to believe.

We also have to use wisdom on how we handle our dominion. We don't go find a dog or a lion and say I have dominion over you, and don't think that you will be alright. God is just saying if you find yourself in harm's way, know that I have your back and you will be okay, because you have authority over the situation.

God is not a dumb God neither will He tell you to do stupid things. Sometimes our bad decisions can turn into a negative outcome. The Bible says you don't test God, that is a sin. When we walk by faith, it does not mean we don't carry wisdom, meaning we leave our brain at home. Some things require you to walk by faith, and some require you to walk by wisdom. Faith is used when you are going through a tough time and you are believing God for an answer of wisdom on how to get through the situation.

For an example, say that you have to put together a major event which you never done before, but you have faith that you can do it. You believe you can get it done, now you will use the wisdom of God, in order to get the details of how to get it done. Details like how you are going to financially support this vision. Who can you ask to help you to put together the vision. You may have to do research on different things you will need in order for the event to be successful. Ask someone that might have done a similar event.

That is how faith and wisdom work hand and hand, you cannot have one without the other. Faith is the action you take and wisdom is how you get it done. Faith is not magic, it is a choice for you to believe something that you cannot see in your current moment. You just have to believe that it is coming. When I wrote my first book, I did not have the money to publish it, but I believed by faith that it was going to be published. I started writing, knowing in my current state that I did not have the funds to guarantee me that I will have a physical book finished, but because I activated my faith by taking action, then, that was when the Lord opened the door for the finance part.

Sometimes God is waiting for you to believe and take action and He is ready to open unusual supernatural doors for you because you believed that He could. Within a year, because I put my faith into action, God provided me the funding to publish my book, and now it is on amazon.com , barnesandnobles.com, on iTunes, and I have my own physical copies I purchased and I even created an audiobook. That is how faith will work in your life.

You believe in something, then you put it into action and the rest will follow. You can't ask God for something, and you don't show Him that you believe Him for it without any action. God only moves by the faith of His children. Even if it does not make sense to do it, do it because God will bless your efforts. He want to see if you are serious about it, before he gets serious about it. The Bible says:

"The LORD will open for you His good treasure house, the heavens, to give rain to your land in its season and to bless all the work of your hand; and you will lend to many nations, but you will not borrow." Deuteronomy 28:12

This verse explains multiple things, for one, on how God blesses His people. He blesses the works of what we put our hands to do. God will give us abundance. God knows what we are in need of, but He knows that it takes us to participate in order to get it done. That is why God gave us the ability to create and prosper. He expects us to use these things. He is only there to help us through it and not do it for us. I am not saying that God cannot perform miracles, which He can and sometimes He does. But miracles only happens if it is out of our power.

For example, healing of your body when the doctors cannot help. We cannot heal ourselves, therefore we pray and ask God to help us. In this example our action for faith is praying. In some cases, you can only pray, and in most cases it is action to receive the blessings of God. But it is always something on our end that we have to do to get God's attention so He can help us.

He also said that there are seasons for everything, so don't be hasty. Don't be in a rush for the blessing because it is coming. We have to be patient, He will open those doors when He knows you are ready for it. The last thing God said in this verse is, as a result of your blessings you will lend and not borrow. You will have so much you can give on another level.

Remember that what God gives us is not only for us, it is also for others. That is why we have to be open to give; some blessings will not come because of our selfishness. When we want it only for selfish reasons and not to give to others, then God is not obligated to open that door. Because the blessing is for a purpose. We have to give with a cheerful heart.

Faith also takes courage; let's take a look at this definition. Courage means the ability to do something that frightens one. It also means strength in the face of pain or grief. Your faith will be challenged, but the courage inside you has to stand up and do it anyway. I know we cannot see it, but when you believe something you cannot see the result of it, that truly is a heart of a person that has an abundance of courage.

It takes a lot to be courageous in situations that you do not know for sure what the outcome will be. I had moments of courage in my life, and I also had moments of cowardliness in my life. I had moments that I confronted my fear and I had moments that I ran from my problems. The reason why I ran is because I allowed fear to be in the forefront. I feared the outcome of what would happen if I confronted it head-on. I felt sometimes that it was going to blow up in my face and I feared that.

For example, when it comes to relationships with people and I felt that it would be a conversation that I would have to face which may turn into an argument, I would avoid having that conversation, because I feared the response of the other party.

There were some moments that I faced my fears, when it came to my life and to make decisions for myself and where I am going, in most cases I would walk in great courage. I am learning now that I have to walk in courage in every area of my life, relationships, business, friendships etc. I am definitely getting better in those areas and I know you have to be consistent in courage. You can be a wimp sometimes and courageous other times. It definitely takes time and practice, you will never be 100% but as long as your taking steps, you are making progress.

Faith is important to our daily lives; it keeps us growing from one level to the next. Without faith, we will stay in the same place for our whole lives and never tap into the potential that God has placed on the inside of us. We need faith, not only to survive, we also need it to thrive, to move into places that we have never been. Faith also will make you uncomfortable; it does not always make you feel good, because it takes you to unfamiliar places.

That is why, when you are believing God for something, you sometimes feel uncomfortable acting on what you are believing God for. If you want to be a man or woman of faith, you cannot stay in comfortable places, because in faith, you are always in a place of movement. You have to adjust because there will always be a change that is taking place in your life when you decide that you will walk by faith and not by sight.

We also have the power to speak faith now. We can believe God to do something for us now; it could be a miracle that you are asking for. It could be something that you worked on like a project or a promotion and you want Him to move on your behalf.

That is an example of now faith because God decided just to give you the desires of your heart. Sometimes, God does operate in 'now' faith, but this is not always the case. God wants you to be patient for His promises. It all depends when God decides to do it now or later. Sometimes we can work so hard on something that God is telling us to do and it takes a long time before you flourish in that area. Sometimes God is testing us to see how diligent you are and can you still believe Him when nothing is happening, and it is just the test of your obedience.

Can you stay where God placed you, can you be faithful and consistent in what He placed in your hands. He wants to see your faith in Him; He wants to know if you believe Him or not. God will have us to wait to build our faith. Or He will hold it up because we may not be ready for what God has for us. He has to prepare us for the BIG, because some of us are not ready. We will destroy what God has helped us create, God wants us to be mature enough to handle it. We believe that we are ready and mature enough, but when testing comes and we fall apart, it shows that we are not ready. The Bible says:

"But his delight is in the law of the Lord, And on his law [his precepts and teachings] he [habitually] meditates day and night. And he will be like a tree firmly planted [and fed] by streams of water, Which yields its fruit in its season; its leaf does not wither; And in whatever he does, he prospers [and comes to maturity]" Psalms 1:2,3

In this verse, God shows how powerful His word is and when we walk in it by faith. That whatever we put our hands to do it will prosper. It also talks about seasons and the timing of God. We have to know that our patience will mature us when the timing is released. We have to also pray and wait on God's timing, He knows what is best for us.

The Bible says:

"Do not be anxious or worried about anything, but in everything [every circumstance and situation] by prayer and petition with

thanksgiving, continue to make your request known to God." Philippians 4:6

We shouldn't be anxious. When we do, it is a sign of immaturity, God is a God of patience, and we must be patient concerning God's plans for our lives. When we are too anxious, the things that we desire can turn into our god, if we are not careful. That is why we have to wait on the Lord and in His perfect timing after we do all we can to get to where God wants us to be.

The Lord has a plan for our lives, but we have to move by faith in order to obtain every promise that God has for us. Having faith in something allows you to see far beyond where you currently are even when it does not look like that is the direction that you are going.

Chapter 4

Hope in your Faith

Faith gives you hope, when it looks like there is no hope at all. Hope means a feeling of expectation and desire for a certain thing to happen. I had moments in my life when I had no money to take care of myself, but I believed God by hoping that I would survive and somehow He was going to provide me funds to take care of my necessities. He sure did, because I had only $2 to my name and living on my own and had to get food.

Someone came to me and put $100 in my hand and this person did not know my financial situation. Only God could have shown them that. I am not saying you should be lazy and wait for handouts, but I am saying when you are in a tough spot, God will see you through, just hope in Him. Sometimes that is all you have, and don't be ashamed that you only just have that. I want to let you know that, that is enough for God to hear your prayer.

God will hear you when you call on him. You may not be able to see it, but you will just know it on the inside of you that He is about to move on your behalf. So you have to believe in everything you do to be successful and grow in your everyday life. Your hope counts, just keep on believing when you cannot see.

You will have doubts, but just know that you cannot stay in that place for long, because it will discourage you, cripple you to a place that you will stop and then you fall into a place of depression, which is not a good place. So, when doubt comes, you tell doubt that you don't have time right now and you are too busy believing God for greater.

Sometimes your past can affect your faith, you cannot move on from your past if you don't have faith. For example, you have a business venture that you went into and it failed. If you don't have enough faith to believe that you can do it again, it will stagnate you, and you will not take another leap because you are dwelling on what happened before. Your past is just a teacher, you don't want your past to be the reason you lack faith, and you want your faith to grow. In order for it to grow, you have to ask God to strengthen you, to move anyway.

You also need faith in order to progress in your life. Without progress, you are not fulfilling your purpose on this earth. You might as well not exist, if you don't fulfill God's purpose of why you are existing. This is not to make you feel bad or start a pity party of saying maybe I should not be here. Yes, you are supposed to be here, that is why God created you. You need to open your eyes and know that God wants more from you than just the same ole same ole. That is a saying that some people say when they are unhappy and don't know who they are.

Purpose is very important, because purpose allows you to walk in the grace of God. Here is what I mean, when you walk in what you were called to do, it won't be hard because you have a special ability in that area. Sometimes, people call it your Super Power. Something that you are so good at that it blows everyone that tries to compete with you out of the water. It is a gift from God that no one can do it like you can. That is what makes you unique. You were destined to do what you are doing and also you feel fulfilled.

Have you ever felt uneasy about a job you took or an assignment that was given and you felt out of place. That is a sure sign that you are not walking in purpose at that moment. Some things are just for a season at times, so I am not telling you to quit your job. But I am telling you to seek God for your purpose that He has called you to, so you won't be locked into a place that God has not called you to. Your faith in God will bring you to your destiny when you seek after your purpose.

Faith cannot work without a vision, you need a vision in faith, meaning, you have to visualize yourself there and have to move by faith on the vision you saw. Before I purchased my first home and when I saw it, I knew it was my desired home because I already envisioned what my first home would look like in my mind. Also, I saw myself watching T.V. in that same house. I almost did not get this house, but my vision kept me thinking that it was my house. I even got to a place, when it looked like it was falling apart, I just had hope, but it was enough for God to turn my situation around. I had to see myself there before I actually possessed it. That is what you have to do.

You have to see yourself already living in it, driving in it, sailing in it, whatever your desire is, it is already yours, you just have to know it is. Visualizing yourself there allows you to build a desire and motivation to get what you want. It allows you to take the proper steps to make it happen in your life. The vision allows you to see it before you see it. It helps you to understand that you can have it, it is already yours even though you do not currently have it in your possession. Your faith allows you to see and visualize your dream. Don't let anyone stop you from believing it is in you to grow by faith. Everything you need is inside of you. You just have to believe that you already have it. The more you believe the more you will grow in what God has created you to be.

Your faith has to be so solid that you still have to believe and be consistent in your goals and dreams even when you don't see anything happening. Faith also takes trying something new even when it does not make sense to anyone but you, and also when you don't have the detailed information or a road map. For example, when I first started my online business coaching, I did not know anything about coaching. This was all new to me, but I knew that this was a door that God wanted me to walk in.

I had enough faith to try because I have a Facebook page for the past 4 years that I did something called "Awaken the new you," 5min of Inspiration with Shakeema S. Perry. So I knew right then God was preparing me for coaching because now I was comfortable speaking live in front of an audience, but at the beginning I was petrified.

God will sometimes have you to do small things to train you to take you to the next level. Sometimes it does not make any sense, but in time, it does make total sense of why God took you in that direction. Even your job, you have a purpose of being there. being a light to your co-workers while you are there. But when it came to coaching I didn't know enough, so God placed a Coach in my life to teach me skills and techniques.

When I was doing my page I was just winging it. But God wanted me to go to a new level in my gifts. I needed more strategies and how to navigate this new venture I entered into. So faith comes with order, you cannot just have faith and no direction and a plan to succeed. It is good to have help in your faith for someone that has the tools you need for your success. This will help you to do it effectively, especially when something is new. In no way am I saying that this applies to every situation, but sometimes God will place people in your life that can help you and sometimes God wants you to take that leap of faith to trust Him to make that next move.

When you are believing God for something big, it takes hard work. It takes time and diligence. Do not give up because it is hard, but you have to work through it even when you don't understand the full picture of what is happening. I know in my life things are sometimes difficult, and to be transparent, I sometimes in the past quit, because it gets very overwhelming, but now God is teaching me endurance because that is the only way to success. Did God quit when He sent His son, Jesus, down to earth because we could not get it together in the world.

Jesus had to go all the way through the process to the cross to die for our sins. Did He quit on us or did He fulfill God's purpose? He fulfilled and finished it. God wants us to be finishers too. That is what God is expecting from us, to go all the way through the process just like Jesus did. He expect us to have the mind of Christ just like in Philippians 2:5. You have to be mentally tough when it comes to having faith, you cannot get stuck in your emotions and what is happening at the current moment.

You have to know that this time in your life is just for a season it will not last forever. It is not in your life to stay, it cannot stay because God will not allow it to stay because you are His child and He loves you and will take care of you. It is only there to train you for the next blessing or position God is going to place you in. It is only there to prepare you for your future.

The things that you faced in your life that you think you lost, don't look at it as a loss, look at it as a gain. Losing is a good thing, when you lose something, it is an opportunity to gain something new. For example, if you lost your job, sometimes that may be an opportunity to start your own business. I know someone who lost her job, started her business and now owns 5 daycare centers because she looked at her loss as a gain. So if she did not lose her job, she would not be in the position that she is in.

Faith is facing whatever obstacle you are going through head-on without allowing fear to stop you and that type of faith is mountain-moving faith. Faith in God is a powerful tool against the enemy. So if you focus on keeping that faith mindset, you will always be a cut above the rest. Faith gives you insight, that is a fear, mindset cannot be revealed. Having your faith constantly exercised is so important for you to have and protect your faith.

Chapter 5

How to Protect your Faith

You protect your faith by keeping your connection with God. Staying in prayer, reading and studying God's word. Doing these things will keep your faith unshakable. When your faith is unshakable, the enemy does not have room to come in. It is like you paralyze him from affecting you and your emotions. He will talk to you but you cannot listen to anything He will say because your faith is so high that it does not matter what He is saying. So you have to also walk in your authority when it comes to your faith.

You have to look at faith as your guide and your GPS. It will take you to the right location every time. Right now I am in a season that God is allowing me to tap into something new. I am in a season that I am transitioning from my job which is paying me almost 60k a year plus bonus and going into Full Time Entrepreneurship. That is pretty good money, but I had to obey God and leave when He told me to, because the Lord has a greater plan for me and my life.

The Lord is very strategic, before leaving He introduced me to a coach that help other coaches to teach what they know and to learn how to Coach and make it a business. She helped me to build an online school to teach my classes. Her name is Shalena Broaster, you actually will hear more from her later on in this book. She is a phenomenal teacher and I am already making thousands of dollars in my Coaching business.

This was something new that I have never done before, which I mentioned earlier, but God purposed me to do this that is why I am flowing in it the way I am. That is what happens when you are in His will and purpose, it flows a little easier than it would if you were not. I am walking by faith, learning new things that I have never tapped into before.

Sometimes in life, when it comes to faith, you may not understand it at first, but it will all make sense later, you just have to obey God in what He wants you to do. So whatever you want to do, don't give up on it, you might have setbacks, but with God, He is setting you up for great success. When you get knocked down, get back up and try again, it will not hurt you to do it, it will actually show you what is on the inside of you. When you don't allow anything to hold you back. This is your preparation for greater things that are about to come in your life. God has more in store than what you think. I know some people feel like God has forgotten them. I know that feeling, I felt like that when I lost my mind because of a traumatic accident when I was 5, I thought God didn't care, but He cares so much about you and He loves you with an everlasting love.

You are never alone God will always be there to care for you, to guide you and protect you no matter what place you are in your life. If you are in your valley experience and you feel that nothing is going your way or at your mountain top experience and things are going pretty good for you. Know that God will keep you in your hardest moments and you will survive no matter what you are going through, He has you in the palm of His hands. I am learning that you are not going to get the reason that you are going through something. Things will just have to unfold of what the outcome will be.

The reason I believe God does that is because He is God and we are not. If we knew everything then why would we need him in our lives? God hides things from us to really protect our heart and our feelings so we will not fall apart. He knows our weakest areas, He knows how to build us up and He knows how to break us down when necessary.

But the Lord does not want to break us down, He really desires to build us up. He knows all about what we are going through, what challenges that we are facing in our lives, and He cares about all of it. In this season of my life, I am being built up mentally by being a Coach and also having a Coach and a Mentor truly is changing my life for the better.

I am so grateful and thankful for all God has done for me thus far. I believe having a Mentor or Coach teaches you that you do not know it all. There are things you have to learn from someone else. That is true humility, when you can recognize that you need help and you do not know everything. That is what I am learning and I am happy about it. So you have to humble yourself to listen to someone that has more knowledge than you. I know that this is not what you want to hear, but it is true.

Humility opens doors and keeps you there. When you are prideful, the opposite of humility, you may go through the door, but you will not be able to stay because somewhere down the line your pride will destroy what you built. You have to listen, compromise, and admit that you are wrong. Pride does not want to do that, and because of that, it will mess up everything that your heart desires. Do you want that? I don't think so, so remember this, just because you don't know it all does not mean you don't know anything, it is just means you are learning and growing. If you look at it like that, it would not be so hard to listen.

I struggled in the area of pride, but God used my Coach to destroy that inner demon in me. How God used her was, she told me what to do in my business, and I was not used to someone telling me what to do. You know the saying "I am grown and no one tells me what to do" that is the spirit of pride. Humility is always ready to be corrected if it is not correct, because a person with humility is excited to grow and learn new things.

A prideful person is stuck in their ways and never grow as a person or as a businesswoman or man. I started to listen to my Coach in just about everything she told me to do in my business and guess what? I made money every time she told me to do something and I did it. I realize that listening has a benefit that comes with it. It is growth, and also helps you not to hit walls that you really did not have to go through when you listen.

I actually made almost 5K in 7 months in my Coaching business. It may not seem like a lot but remember I never did this before so who can say they made that much money learning something new. Remember I was leaving my job, I can learn how to maximize my money on even a greater scale based on all the knowledge I gain.

Each level takes a greater level of faith, because it is a new thing or new to you. Every place that God takes you, you have to hear the Holy Spirit and follow His lead. He will never steer you in the wrong direction. Keep on fighting and protecting your faith. Don't let the devil or anyone steal that from you.

When it looks like nothing is happening in your life and you are working to make something happen, keep on doing the work, because God has something greater for you when you move by faith and still trust Him no matter what you see in front of you. You will start to see a shift in your life when you keep going by working on your vision that God gave you. I like to call this the blessing shift; this means that as you keep trusting God, He will start to lift the burden of your pain and overflow you with His blessings.

It can be as simple as God's peace, meaning that the blessing that you want from God is just peace from your chaotic situation. That is God's blessing shift. He gives you what you need when you need it. There are other blessings that He gives His children when you trust Him with everything and that was just an example of one.

I woke up one morning just thinking about my life and my journey with God. I have given my heart to the Lord for 15 years now. Wow, time sure enough flies. I looked over my Christian walk, and I realize something, that every big decision and even some small ones I have made was always led by God, and me moving by Faith in Him. I just want to share a few and you can read it all in my Autobiography "The Mind Regulator" you can go to gleebargaincenters.com to get your signed copy. But anyway I moved from New York to Richmond with my car and my clothes without having a job set up and I trusted God.

With me moving by faith I got an apartment with no Job. The job He provided paid me double compared to the one I had in New York and so many wonderful things that God has done. This all happened by faith, if I did not take the faith steps I did, I would still be in New York in the same place I was struggling, because that was what was happening almost 8 years ago. God has kept me this long and He can also keep you when you believe Him for the impossible to be made possible.

One more thing was writing my first book with no money to publish it. I listen to God writing it and He provided the money to publish my book. You see how that works acting and then God moves. Sometimes we say we are waiting on God, but most of the time, He is waiting for us to move and trust Him. You see the pattern in this message I trusted God in all my decisions I made in Him and I was always successful in it. I obeyed His voice when He told me to move. I am no different than you, the only difference is I just listened to God and followed His instructions that is how I got to the place I am now.

You can do the same thing but it would be a different path, because we all have our own path to walk. So if you say that I am following God now and nothing is happening, my suggestion is to keep on following what He told you to do and your day is coming. Trust me I went through a long process before God started opening doors for me quickly. It took some time and growth for God to trust me with the things that I have now.

I waited for 7 years when my mind was tormented and I lost it, because of a childhood accident. I had to wait on God, and so do you, but wait and work in great expectation that He is going to do it just for you. It is tailored made and it just fits you and no one else. So if you thought God forgot about you, He did not. Everything has a season attached to it, it is a season for everything. Read the book of Ecclesiastes, it will tell you about seasons. So when your season comes, nobody can stop it, manipulate it or even know when it will happen for you. That is God's secret and surprise that He wants to give you in your life.

 The only person that can stop that season is you, when you don't follow God's instructions and you quit. If He tells you to do something, do it, even when it doesn't make sense to you, just do it. Like start writing your book, or apply for that new promotion, or volunteer at a homeless shelter. When God tells you to do something, in most cases, it is a set up for you and a set up for someone else.

Your breakthrough is not only for you, it is to help someone else or multiple people. That is why some things are on hold. It just cannot only benefit you, it has to benefit people around you and beyond. That is why you must take action on your part, your blessings will not come automatically.

You have to play your part in this life to be successful and it will all happen in God's timing. You have to be sensitive enough to the Holy Spirit to hear God clearly of the timing of when to do something, especially if it is a major move in your life. But say for example you move too early it is ok, because all experience in life is a teacher so don't worry. If you fail at it, because God knows where you are and He will redirect you to the place that you are supposed to be.

God would rather you move and fail than do nothing, because what you are doing is that you are showing God that you trust

Him and He honors that. So don't look at this as a bad thing because the journey you took was not in vain, it was only preparation for your future. I have done plenty of things out of God's timing, thinking it was God, but it was for my benefit, because it did not stop me. It showed me that it was coming but not just yet and I learned from the mistakes I have made and all it did is make me better and a stronger woman.

For example, I have dated multiple men not at the same time, but through the years of being single, that I thought was my husband and come to find out they were not. But I had to date them to find that out, I would have never known if I did not take action. But those experience made me better it showed me what type of man I don't want. You have to go through things sometimes to identify what you don't want in something, then you will understand what you do want.

The men that I dated was not driven like I was and did not have that relationship with God like I did. Those things were important to me so it would not work, I will not just settle for anyone I will have to see the fruits of the Holy Spirit to know if he is the one. I know that sounds deep, but I don't want to be in divorce court multiple times because I ignored the signs because I just wanted a man. I'm sorry God has better than that for me.

So everything you go through, there is a lesson to learn. Some of us go through life hitting the same brick wall and don't learn anything. The way to overcome that bad experience is to look at the good in every situation because it can always be worse. So know when you get a no from God or it is signs that it is a no, don't look at it as a no-look at it as a not yet. Just accept the no and wait for your yes, because it is coming.

Sometimes I have feared hearing the word no, because I did not like being rejected. Then I started to realize if I don't take risks in life, I would never know what the results would have been, but if I took that leap of faith, I would. At this point in my life I do not want regrets, that is why I am now walking in full time entrepreneurship with my head held high knowing that God said for me to go full time and He will keep me all the way through it. He has done it before in my life, and I know He will do it again.

I will not go under in this, I will succeed by the grace of God and my faith that I have in Him and my abilities to turn my business into not only 6 figure but 7 figure and beyond. I trust God that much for my future. Do you believe that for yourself? If you don't, you need to start believing God for the big in your life. You have to start by changing the perspective of who you are. You are God's child, you are a King's kid which means you are royalty and you are unstoppable. You have to see yourself that way because the enemy is ready to tear your self-esteem down.

But don't allow him, you protect your faith with your words that you say to yourself. Know what God thinks about you and say about you in His word. That is how you overcome every obstacle that tries to destroy your life. You have to know that the God you serve, he is powerful, the ruler of the earth and the earth is in His possession and God has given you dominion over it, because you are His child. The Bible says:

"The earth is the Lord's and the fullness of it, the world and those who dwell in it." Psalms 24:1

These are the types of scriptures you should read to build that faith in you to believe more and for greater things in your life. So walk in your authority daily, and you will start to see your life change right before your eyes. It is going to blow your mind and everyone that is connected to you. You will be amazed what God can do when you have faith in Him. He honors your faith. In the Bible, many times, Jesus said that your faith has made you whole, also God was pleased with Abraham's faith. He was called the father of many nations. That goes to show you that God truly honors faith, because it is impossible to please him without it. That is what the Bible says:

"But without faith it is impossible to [walk with God and] please Him, for whoever comes [near] to God must [necessarily] believe that God exists and that He rewards those who [earnestly and diligently] seek Him." Hebrews 11:6

So you understand that God holds faith in high esteem, because that is the only way to please Him. Another requirement to please God is to live a holy life unto Him. That is being righteous toward God and not being perfect but striving to be more like His son daily. What do I mean? You have to live the word of God, no profanity, no sex before marriage, no sex with other people while you are married, no stealing, and no homosexual lifestyle.

These are just some of them. But what God wants from us is to not to do these things and even if we do these things, we can repent and turn away from these things that are not of Him. We cannot call ourselves Christians with the mindset that you can love God and do anything you want. it does not work that way. The Bible says:

"But first and most importantly seek (aim at, strive after) His kingdom and His righteousness [His way of doing and being right—the attitude and character of God], and all these things will be given to you also." Matthew 6:33

The first requirement is holiness and then God adds His blessings to you. Yes, it is guidelines to what God has for you. It is your faith and obedience, it goes hand in hand. So you have to remember that you have to please God before the promise of blessings that He will release on your life. Not being perfect, because none of us will be but giving an effort to live right and please Him. Be the best son or daughter you can be.

You like what He likes and you hate what He hates. That is why as a Christian man or woman, you have to stay in God's word. That is our instruction book for our lives, how we are supposed to act, think and do. The reason some Christians don't follow the word of God, because they don't read or study or know what it says about us. The Bible says:

"I will worship toward thy holy temple, and praise thy name for thy lovingkindness and for thy truth: for thou has magnified thy word above thy name." Psalms 138:2

That is how much God honors His word, that He magnified it higher than himself. So this scripture exemplifies that He takes His word very seriously and He expects us to honor it as well. We sometimes take God's word lightly and we pick and choose what we want to believe and follow, but the Bible says eat the whole scroll, that just means believe the whole word and follow it to the best of your ability and when you struggle, ask God to help you because He will.

When we don't attempt to follow God's word, that is when some of the prayers we prayed has not been answered yet, because we have to get right with God first. We cannot see the promises of God when we don't keep our promise to obey His word. So if you are not following God's word, I behoove you to do so, because it will stop you from receiving your full potential of blessings from God. You may see sprinkles but you will not see the whole thing. God is only obligated in the word to supply all of your needs according to His riches in glory, but the promises of God comes with requirements on your part.

This includes me as well, I had to obey God's word in order to get where I am today. What I mean by that a lot of things was revealed to me by the Holy Spirit to order my steps to where I am now. I did not get to a place of getting my mind back, being a business owner of 3 companies, being a homeowner and so much more by myself. If I did not obey the Lord, He would not allow me to hear the mysteries of Christ.

I had to walk holy before God, not perfect but always having the heart to do right and please Him. Until this day, I have been celibate for 14 years and I am still waiting on my husband. That is what I mean, not falling into temptation because it feels good. So if you are someone that made a mistake God will forgive you, but at some point you cannot keep doing something and ask for forgiveness because you are not really sorry, if you continue in it, it may turn to an addiction and if it is, ask God to deliver you from that spirit of addiction.

God has so much for us we just have to know He does and listen to Him and what He is saying we should do. It is not easy being celibate, I can tell you that, but I love God and want to please him more than my desires. Trust me if I was intentionally in sin I will not have had half of the testimonies I have told you. That is why you must not only love God but fall in love with Him, meaning the presence of God. His holy spirit that can wrap His arms around you anytime you feel stress, depress, angry and anything that may be dampening your spirit.

So living right is for all of us, no one is exempted from doing the right thing toward God. The Bible says, the rain falls on the just and the unjust. I don't know about you, but I want to be on the side of the just, and that is God's side and His people. I want everything that God has for me, don't you? That is the question that you have to ask yourself daily, I will let you just ponder on that for a moment.

So I wanted to go back to walking in this life when it comes to walking by faith in God. Your life as a Christian revolves around faith. Every step and everything you do has to go by what you don't see by your natural eye. You have to look beyond the natural and see in the spirit. How do you do that you may ask? You do that by spending time with your creator, it is that simple. The more you nurture your relationship with God the more that He will reveal Himself to you. You grow your relationship with Him through prayer, reading and studying His word and sometimes just having a conversation.

At the beginning of your walk with God, sometimes it is not very clear, but eventually God starts speaking to you in His own unique way, and you start to hear Him much clearer.

That is how I started out, I did not understand how to hear God and understand if He is speaking to me or not, but over time it all make sense and I understood His language and how He speaks to me. He can directly speak to you and you can hear His voice, He can speak to you in your mind, you can feel when He speaks to you by a touch, also this is a big one that's we don't like, He can speak to us through people. Yes, there are so many ways God can get our attention when He is talking to His children. But you will know in time based on if you build a relationship with Him or not.

You will never know everything about God, I know I do not but it is just like a relationship with a person the more you are around them the more you get to know them. It is the same thing with God, you just don't physically see Him. The more you build with him the more confident you become in him and you know that He cannot lie and He will always be there for you and He will never leave you nor forsake you. I know that with God, because we have a strong relationship and I know that He will come through for me.

That is what you call a relationship and experience that is what builds your faith over time. God has an excellent track record with me, He has won every fight for me. He has never failed me yet, and He never will, and He will not fail you either.

Faith is not visible, so when you talk to people about faith and they don't believe or they have limited faith, they tend to tear your faith down. The reason is that they don't understand the concept of faith and how it works and how it can work for you and them. So what happens if you tell the wrong person your faith moves in God? Your dreams and goals that you desire to do. This is what would happen, maybe not intentionally, they will start to eat away at your faith with the words that they will say.

For example say you are believing God for a house and you have bad credit, so someone with lack of faith would say how can you afford a mortgage you don't make that much money at your job. Also, they would say it is hard to get that credit straight and it is better to rent because when you buy you have to pay for your own maintenance. Just with those words alone, it will start to plant doubt in your mind, and if you hear the negativity enough you will talk yourself out of your dream.

That is why you have to protect your faith, you sometimes have to keep the dream to yourself until you get the keys then open your mouth. Sometimes the enemy use people as a distraction so you won't get all that God has for you.

I know in 2015 I wanted to get a house, and I told a friend not intentionally she wanted to discourage me, because she was a homeowner herself and she knew what it was like to own a home. She told me to wait until I was married because the maintenance can get expensive. She did not know, but after that conversation I talked myself out of getting my home that year, because I believed her. She did not do It on purpose she was only trying to protect me, but you have to be very careful not to release your dream in the atmosphere prematurely.

Sometimes you have to keep it between you and God, because that is the safest place, especially when you are believing God for the big. Some people may not understand that, because some dreams are too big for people so sometimes you have to keep them to yourself. But not everyone want to intentionally kill your dreams they are just human like you and sometimes want the best for you. But your journey may be different from theirs, and they just don't understand your journey with God.

You want to make sure when you are working and going through a tough process, oh yes, it gets real tough sometimes. That you do not have any outside influence that is not in the direction that God is telling you to go. You don't want to blame anyone for your failures but you, you want to make sure that you hear God for clear instructions. If you mess up, you can only blame yourself not feeling guilty but knowing that you have to make the necessary adjustments in order to make your situation successful.

A lot of time, as people, we want to blame someone else for our mistakes and failures because we don't want to take responsibility on our part. We have to learn that we must take responsibility for all the actions we take as well. I am not saying you can't tell nobody your dreams, I am just saying try to get God's permission first. I did not do that, I was just excited and I shared something out of time. Thank God in 2017 I got the house and I did not tell anyone until close to closing and the same person helped me to believe and celebrated me all the way. So she was not bad, I just released it too early.

Know that only you can stop you, no one else. So you have to put your grown pants on and get back in the game even when someone might have talked you out of it or you talked yourself out of it. It really doesn't matter who did what all that matters is that you don't quit and give up on your dreams and yourself. You have to fight for what you really want, do you want it bad enough to fight for it. You can only stop yourself from stepping in your destined place.

Do it in fear if you have to, because fear is a feeling, not the result of you taking action. Remember feelings come and go and know that you walking by faith can actually change your life forever. So know if you still do it in fear, that fear will completely go away. After the feeling, because you did it anyway, then God's favor will rest upon you because you believed Him anyway in spite of what you felt. So you need to take your shield of faith and walk in total victory without regrets.

Chapter 6

Faith is the Evidence

This chapter came from the book of Hebrews 11:1 it says,

"Now faith is the assurance (title deed, confirmation) of things hoped for (divinely guaranteed), and the evidence of things not seen [the conviction of their reality - faith comprehends as fact what cannot be experienced by the physical senses]."

I was in my room, and God brought this verse to my spirit in prayer. He said that faith is the evidence. For example, if I leave my finger print on my wall, can I see the finger print? No, probably if I get a fluorescent light on it, then I can see it, right? So that is what God was showing me, that you don't have to see your faith, but it is all the evidence you need to walk in your destiny and your purpose in Him.

When you have true faith in God, you don't need to see everything to know that it is there. God gives us glimpses of our future for a reason. He knew that we needed something to keep us headed toward what He is saying for us to do so we can get to a place of it manifesting in the natural.

The vision that God gives us is an image that is not tangible yet. You have to have faith in that vision and continue to trust God and allow Him to lead you and instruct you so you will actually see that vision in your life. If you believe that your faith is the evidence, you will start to understand what a faith walk is all about. I believe that when you walk with God, it is truly a faith walk. Why do I say that?

This is true because we cannot see God, so we would have to believe He is there when we cannot see Him. That is why I said that faith is your evidence because God is a spirit that we cannot see, but my faith is the evidence that He does exist and He is real. He lives within me through the Holy Spirit, and He works through me.

He is also driving the key points that I am driving to you in this book. Nothing can exist without faith; everything that was created on the face of the earth was through faith. Just read the book of Genesis where it talks about the Lord who spoke the world into existence by faith. When He said, let there be light. God believed that light was going to appear when He said it. Even God knew His faith was His evidence. He knew that he was able to speak things into existence by His faith, believing once He spoke it, then He was going to see it right before His eyes.

God has given us that same power. He is God, of course; we cannot do it exactly like Him. We are like God, so he has given us the ability to speak things into existence. Meaning if we desire something that is in the will of God, we have to speak it first because God hears your prayer, and He will answer your call. He will lead and guide you to that promise, sometimes it can be a phone call you will have to make, or God will send someone to you, or it can be an opportunity that opens up that will lead you to that answered prayer.

But overall, God has given us that same power, but we have to follow the path that He wants us to take to achieve the blessings that he has for us. Sometimes it can happen supernaturally by way of a miracle. It is truly up to God and how He wants to bless us. But we can't think that everything will be a miracle; most of the time, it is not. Most things that God has for us will take us acting on our part; if everything was on God alone, He would not have given us a brain to function on the earth and the freedom of choice.

Our brain is supposed to be used to think and be creative and come up with concepts and strategies, also educating ourselves in areas that we don't know sometimes, it may be free education, but sometimes we have to pay for a Coach or Mentor to get it done. Whatever it takes is based on our desires, and if we really want it, we will do what it takes to get it done if we want it. In life, things are not just handed to you; you have to work for them. Also, God allowed that because at the end of the day, if it was just given to you, you would probably not appreciate it. I wouldn't appreciate it as much if I did not work for it.

It is something about when you work hard for something, you have a different posture about it than if it was given for free. When it is given free, it is looked upon as not valuable. God wants us to look at the things that He has for us as valuable, not tossed to the side. Some of us are not ready for God to perform miracles when he does; we would take it for granted. So God knows when to do something and when not to do something. That is why we have to use our faith as evidence that God is on our side, that we will get through any hard time in our lives. That trouble doesn't always last because God loves us, and He will see us through it all.

We have nothing to be afraid of; we have the strongest force in the universe protecting us from the evil of this world. Our confidence in God needs to be built up as we grow in Christ. God cares for our well-being. He cares for our life. He just wants His children to trust Him more and stop worrying about things that will last for just a little while. As people, we worry too much about things that may never happen. How about we concentrate on things that will happen great in our lives, not the opposite. If we spend more time focused on the positive things that God has done, we will not focus on the negative that the enemy had done. The Bible says:

"The thief comes only in order to steal and kill and destroy. I came that they may have life, and have it in abundance [to the full, till it overflows]."

John 10:10

It is the enemy's job to try to deceive you into believing that God is not on your side and your life is limited when your life is actually unlimited. God has given you an unlimited mind to believe Him for whatever is in your heart. God has a greater plan than you can ever imagine; he is waiting for you to acknowledge it and believe that it is for you.

He has many blessings that He wants to give, but the enemy has clouded your mind and you sometimes start to believe his lie and cannot receive God's truth about you. God has a good scripture that you can study that talks about the power that you possess that you may not know you have. The Bible says:

"Listen carefully: I have given you authority [that you now possess] to tread on serpents and scorpions, and [the ability to exercise authority] over all the power of the enemy (Satan); and nothing will [in any way] harm you." Luke 10:19

So know that God stands by His Word, and He has given you and I the power to destroy the works of the enemy, and do you know where the enemy attacks you the most? He attacks you the most in your mind because he has your life if he has your mind. You probably saying to yourself, how? Here is a good example, where does an idea come from? Your mind right, so say, for example, you have an idea to build a cruise line, and you want to make it different from all the cruise lines that are out now. So you thought of what you want to do.

Now you have to figure the how to do it, then doubt comes in and tells you how you would come up with the money for something that big? You have never done this before. Do you have enough knowledge to get this done? So all of these thoughts randomly go through your mind. Then you start to believe those thoughts; what happens to your idea? It starts to get smaller and smaller until you don't want to do it anymore. Get the idea, the enemy spoke to your mind enough that he stole your life. Not your physical life but your life's dream. Do you understand my point?

That is why faith has to be at the forefront. It has to be your solid evidence that you will accomplish everything that you set your heart to do. Don't believe the enemy or your own thoughts; believe what God has spoken to you through His Word. You will see your life change when you do. God has major for your life, and He is ready to bless you BIG!! So don't let any thought in your mind stop you from walking in the faith that God has placed on the inside of you. So know that your faith is all the evidence you need to get all that God has for you.

Chapter 7

Faith has No Restrictions

When you think of faith, what do you think about, and what do you see? How do you view faith? Do you look at it like faith works sometimes and sometimes it doesn't? Well, I want to let you know that faith has no restrictions; it is not in a box. You can sometimes have faith in something and, it may not happen. One of the reasons this could happen it may be a blessing that God will give you later that He will release at the right time.

Another reason is that it could be that it was not his will for you to have it, but it does not mean that your faith was restricted. It just means that God is the pilot, and you are the co-pilot of your faith. God determines the outcome, but He still expects you to believe Him for what you desire for your life.

He may take you through a detour of your faith, but you will get to the destination of what He desires for your life. He has done that to me, I always wanted to be an actress and move to Hollywood, but God had different plans for me. I had faith in it and was going to do it at the age of 23. But God knew that my journey wasn't that route. He took me through a detour and showed me my real purpose in business. I started to understand why God did not want me in Hollywood based on the things that goes on, but I started to see the business in me as I kept living. But I still believe in some way I am connected to Hollywood but to minister to the lost souls in that industry.

What I like about God, He knows us in and out, and my call is in ministry and business, and now I am a full-time entrepreneur who owns 3 companies and doing well. At this time in my life, I will always take God's plans over mine because He knows what's best for me. God is simply amazing in the things He does in our lives. We just want to know every detail, but that is not faith. Faith does not know every detail; we just have to know enough to move step by step while following God and letting Him lead us.

That is true faith; walking blindly with the Holy Spirit even when you do not know all the details. Details are good, but sometimes too many details can scare you, for example, what if God told you that you were going to have a car accident, then you were going to break your leg. Then after a long 5 year battle in court, you will win a million-dollar lawsuit. That would be too much information, I think. I would not want to know about all the suffering I would go through to get to that million dollars. Isn't that too many details?

That is why God only reveals pieces of the details and the outcome of the situation because He does not want to scare you. Also, you will not want to go through that process because too much was revealed to you. He hides things from us for a reason, which is, we cannot handle everything that we think we can handle. It is too much for us to bear. That is why we have the promise word from God to keep us in faith, keep us focus and to stay encouraged by the Word He gave us. But we have to go through the process for the promise. So if we go through the process of life challenges, hurt, pain etc., we eventually will see the promise that God has set up for us.

Faith is powerful because it keeps you at peace even when a storm in your life is raging. The Word that God has given you overrides what you see and feel for that moment. Remember it is just a moment that you are feeling, so you have to know it will not last long. You got to keep the faith and hold on to God's Word and what He promised you. So you will not fall into doubt, fear, worry, discouragement, and then ultimately depression. That is why God's Word is important to have in your heart no matter what. The Bible says:

"Your word I have treasured and stored in my heart, that I may not sin against you".

Psalms 119:11

When you have God's Word hid in your heart, it will take you down a path that you don't sin against God. Not saying you will be perfect because I am not, but you will do your best not to sin in order to please God. Do you know that doubt is a sin? Yes, it is; the Bible says that it is impossible to please Him without faith. What is the opposite of faith? Doubt. So know that when you doubt, that it is not pleasing to God. But when the Word is hidden in your heart, that will help you stay in a faith mode that you will not doubt but believe what God has spoken to you.

You know that some of us had prophetic words spoken to us over the years, and some of us still have not seen the manifestation of those words in our lives. Some of the reason why that happens is timing, obedience, and faith. Timing means that God is not releasing it now, you may be working toward something, but it will be released in the time you want. Disobedience would be you are not living the life God wants you to live; you are living out of the will by running after your own lust and not what God has set up for you. Not using your faith by doubting and not take the necessary steps for God to move by the works of your hands.

We have to ask God the question of what I am supposed to be doing in this season? Have we ever just in prayer asked God that question? Some of us can say yes, and a lot of us probably would say no, because sometimes we do not think of that Including myself. What do we do? Should we just keep going through the motions of life? If you build a strong relationship with God, sometimes He will tell you directly, or sometimes He will give you signs on what to do.

Either way, God is speaking to us daily, but are we not listening. So we have to be observant of everything that is happening around us, so we will not miss God's move. I don't ever, if it is in my power, want to miss the move of God in my life. His direction in my life is too important for me to be asleep. I want it all; I don't want any crumbs; I want the whole cake.

God has shown me so many things that He wants me to do, and I will make sure that I complete it until I take my last breath on this earth. I believe that God wants to do the same for you. But you have to be willing to go through the process and path that God has you on in this time in your life. It does not matter how painful, hurtful or scary it may be.

Go for all that God has for you because the Holy Spirit is with you through it all. You are more than a conqueror through Christ Jesus. So there will never be a restriction when it comes to your faith in God. Be encouraged that your faith can take you anywhere where God wants you to be; there is no limit. You are walking in unlimited faith; you just don't know it yet, because everything has not been revealed in your life. Faith is not seen. It is something you have to believe.

So, walk the path of your faith, then you will start to see bit by bit things that God has shown you in the spirit, and it starts to manifest in your life. You will be surprised at what you will start to see when you follow that path that God will take you on. It will blow your mind of what God has in mind regarding your life and destiny. I know He blew my mind tremendously with the things that have transpired in my life.

Even though I have been through some real tough times growing up. God remembers every pain and suffering that you go through, and He will reward you for all that you've been through.

When you are going through the path that God has set for you, know that He is rooting for you by the faith that you have in Him. The more that you believe Him, the more that He is pleased with you, and you will accomplish everything that He has for your life. The Bible says:

"I know the plans and thoughts that I have for you, says the Lord, plans for peace and well-being and not for disaster, you and give you a future and a hope." Jeremiah 29:11

God has a blessed outcome for all of us, but we have to believe it before we see it in our lives through faith.

Chapter 8

Faith is the Door

Faith is the gateway to our blessings and favor that God has for us. If we look at faith as our door, we will see faith in a clearer way. Faith is our evidence that the door is right in front of us. We have to visualize it in our minds first before the faith of what we see manifests in our daily lives. Don't get discouraged when you don't see what is in your minds right away because faith has to take its course and hit the natural in time, but it is based on us following the path to where God is directing us to go.

If we don't follow that pathway, we will not see the vision come to reality in our lives, but if we walk with God and not before Him, then we will start to see the pathway of faith clearer, and we will start to see victory after victory in our lives. I am not saying that you will not face some obstacles, but it will not be so hard because you are not doing it alone; God is walking with you.

That is the strongest place to be when the Holy Spirit is backing you up in the spirit realm. So when you move in the Holy Ghost, it starts to work in your favor. Even when other people got a no, you will get a yes. In some cases, you can hear a no, but it does not mean it is over; this sometimes means not yet. That means that God is working behind the scenes on your behalf, and you may get that yes later. Sometimes we are not ready for that blessing yet. Look at your faith the right way; it will take you to a new place in your mind to be unlimited in you through patience. You will start to see things in your life shift for the better.

A shift means to move or cause to move from one place to another. That means if you shift, you're thinking you can move from one tax bracket to another just with that one slight movement. That is how powerful faith is. Just with one small shift in your mind, you can change your life forever. Faith is that impactful; you would have no idea if you don't use it. I know in my life, faith sometimes was all I had, when my mind was tormented for 7 years. I did not have anything to stand on but my faith. My friends, family nobody, could help me but God. You can read more of my story in my book "The Mind Regulator" It captures my full story.

I know that God is my rock and my fortress, and I can't see Him, but I have to believe He exists through my faith. That is why I said that faith is the door. I know the Bible says that faith is the key that unlocks the door, but also, without the door, where would the key go into. So the key and the door intertwine to open up; they are both connected.

I am so excited that God chose me to walk this path of faith. I don't need to know everything. All I need to know from God is my next step and for Him to guide me where He desires me to go. To also please Him with my obedience. That is what makes my heart glad, it has nothing to do with things, but God is pleased with my walk, talk, and how I act. That is why that is one of the reasons that God blesses me the way He does. But it is truly His grace and mercy over my life and yours that does it, but I also believe that your play a part when God releases the blessings through your maturity as well. My heart just wants to please God, which matters to me more than what He gives me any day. The Bible says:

"For the Lord God is a sun and shield; The Lord bestows grace and favor and honor; No good thing will he withhold from those who walk uprightly". Psalms 84:11

So that scriptures shows the why behind the blessings of His people, and I am so excited about it. We have to take ourselves out of the situation and concentrate on God and what he has done already and how he kept you. If you focus on that, then your faith will start to emerge inside of you, that you never thought you had.

I want to let you know that we all have a measure of faith, but as you keep on believing God through time, your faith gets built up and starts to get stronger. It is not an overnight process to believe on great levels. It is a building with God from one level to another. The more you see God move in your life, the more you will believe and trust God for the bigger.

That is how my faith was built; it was not overnight. So you can breathe now, because some are probably thinking that, wow! She believes God like that. The answer is yes, but it definitely took some time to get there. Your experience with God helps you to build that strong mindset of faith. In the beginning, I was scared to death because I was just learning God through His Word and how He did things. I did not have anything to go by, but now 15 years in, my God has the most incredible track record EVER!! I love Him and trust Him with all my heart.

I know that I have strong faith now, but as I said, it was a process of some rough times that I have been through to build this type of faith that I have with God. That is what you will need to do to be in this place of faith. When you go through trials of life, which you will, you will start to see where you are in your faith by your response, and that is good to know where you are so you can continue to build with God. By connecting to God and his Word. We all need a closer walk with God, myself included. But it is good to see where we are in God so we will make proper adjustments in our lives, so we can start to build our faith in God to be the unstoppable man or woman of God that we are because we are tough and built to last. So faith is our door, and we must use our faith every day.

Chapter 9
Building your Faith

How to build your faith is a process. I have been born again, surrendered my life over to Christ for a long time now. I have made mistakes, have I had faithless moments? Absolutely, Have I stayed in those moments? No, I did not. Why did I not stay there? Because moments like the moments I had, was exactly what it was, a moment. Difficulties in your life is only for a moment. Some are longer than others. I had to learn that on my journey with God that trouble doesn't last always.

That is the key when you start to doubt God; it is like going on vacation; you are not going for a long time, you have to come back home, right? So doubt cannot stay; it is not your home. Faith is your home; that is where you reside all year. So that is how you would have to look at your current circumstance; it is not forever.

All of us get scared sometimes, but the most successful people are people that don't stay scared. Also, they have to do it scared, and that is what you have to do sometimes. Remember, fear is just a feeling it comes, and it goes, but once you take that faith step, you start to realize that the fear you had ceased. That is how you overcome your fear. Fear will always be there. Are you going to let fear be your vacation or your home? It was times that I did things, and I did not know what I was doing or know what would be the outcome of my action. But I trusted God was leading me down that path, so I did it anyway, and because I trusted God, the outcome was blessed and successful.

I want to let you know this about me, and what I believe, that I cannot be successful without God point-blank. If you think differently, that is up to you. Because I know a lot of people that are in the world who are successful without God. But the only difference between them and myself is that their success was most likely harder to get and took them more years than they would have had to because they did it on their own. But when you have, God He will give you mysteries that man does not know to get you there faster than you would be able to do alone. The Bible says:

"That is, the mystery which was hidden [from angels and mankind] for ages and generations, but has now been revealed to His saints (God's people)." Colossians 1:26

God can show you strategies of getting wealth without going through the process blindly. There is a benefit in knowing God, it is not for selfishness, but it is to give to people and give God glory. The Bible also says that the Lord give you the power to get wealth. So God knows all and sees all, why not let Him walk you through the process His way instead of the hard way.

Yes, you have to change your ways and be obedient to His Word, but that is worth more than gold. Because you are safe with God and have a place in heaven with Him. That is the difference that you will have with God or without Him because any selfish ambition will not get rewarded from God.

So even if you know it or not, without believing in God through Jesus Christ, you have disqualified yourself from being accepted in God's heavenly kingdom. The Bible says: *"Not everyone who says to Me, 'Lord, Lord,' will enter the kingdom of heaven, but only he who does the will of My Father who is in heaven."* Matthew 7:21

So you see, just because you acknowledge God does not mean you are going to heaven. You have to confess Jesus Christ as Lord and also do the will of the Lord. I know this is getting deep, but all of this is true, if you believe it or not. So if you don't accept Christ, you have automatically accepted the devil as your Lord without even knowing it. Accept Jesus in your heart today, and He is willing to forgive you and take you down this beautiful road with Him and give you the life that He intended for you to live.

I want you to prosper. That is why I must tell you the truth. You have to choose in this life who you are going to serve to see God in heaven. So the choice is truly up to you.

I decided a long time ago to choose Jesus Christ as my Lord and Savior. That is why I am so successful, not because I knew everything. This was a life that God guided me through to walk in the spirit of excellence and to walk in abundance. Success is not only money; it is relationships, health, peace, and just being successful in every area of your life can only be done through God because He helps you to get to that place. I am telling you this based on my experience with God, we all have to run our own race, but I hope you run it with the Lord, because that is a race that you will always win.

This is a way to build your faith as well to make a decision to walk with God no matter what, also to get into more details about building your faith is reading God's Word and not only reading it, also ask God for the understanding of His Word. God's Word can be interpreted in so many different ways, but He will show you what you need to know in the time you need to know it through His Word. I know He does that with me. I can read the same scripture one year and then read it 5 years later and get a different meaning. God shows you revelation through His Word in what you need to see when you need it.

I know that God's Word always encourages me and bless me all the time. Another way of building your faith is to spend time talking to God, let Him know your concerns even though He already knows what you are going through. He still wants you to express what you are feeling to Him, so He can comfort you and direct you in what to do or how to handle your situation. Also, praying for others, you are not the only one going through there are so many others that are going through far more worse than you are.

This will also allow you to have compassion in your heart for other people. It will also make you sensitive to people and their feelings, this is what God loves and this shows maturity and growth. This walk with God is not about only you, it is about others also. I love maturity in God because when you are mature, God knows you are ready for His blessing and also the big blessings that He wants to give us.

So when you start to build your relationship with God, don't make it super complex, just spend 10-15 min per day and then build from that, then over time, increase that time, and then you get to a point you have spent an hour or even hours with Him. That is how that works. You have to build to that place.

Then when you continue to build this with Him, He starts to reveal some things about your life and future. This will be more relational with God at this time because now it is not you looking at the clock; you now want to be in His presence and get God's attention. He will show you what is Him and what is not Him, like people you are around, bad habits, and even places that He does not want you to go no more. What He wants you to do for Him concerning ministry. It is a sacrifice, but a good one. It is a beautiful walk, and I love it!!

It is that deep, but it is training you for His will and the path He is taking you. You are getting better in God and your faith, even though it may not feel like that at the very beginning, but as you continue to walk that path, it will all make sense later. We were never meant to know everything; we just need to know enough to trust and follow God. We have to continue to build our faith by building our relationship. The more we build, the more confidence in God and what He is saying to us.

 Don't be afraid of faith; embrace it like a close friend. Trust me, you are going to need it with every bit of you. I know you may not feel that right now, but later you will. My dad said, if you have not gone through anything, just keep on living. He sure was right about that; you will have to lean and depend on God for your life. Because it is tough out here in these streets. Many people walk around like they don't need God, but deep down inside, they are scared to death, but some of them will never admit that because soon as trouble hit, they do not know what to do, and the first thing they do is cry out too is God.

That is why we need God in our lives; he is our rock in a weary land. Right now, this land is weary; we are still fighting this pandemic, Covid-19, that has killed over 300,000 + people in the U.S and over 1 million worldwide, and those numbers will go up. People are dying rapidly every day, and some of us will still say that we don't need God. We need God more than ever at this point.

This World Crisis happened for a reason, and I believe one of the reasons was to draw us closer to Christ and wake us all up as Christians and the world; our time is limited on this earth. It is also the judgment upon the world because a lot of us forgot about God and our creator and went after other gods, like people, sex, drugs, alcohol, our family, wife, husband, you name it.

We made other people our gods and did not even know it. You may say how? Who do you spend the most time with, and do not spend any time with God? That is how you make other things your God. God knows that you have to live your life, but to build a relationship with Him, you have to have set time with Him daily and some things in our life we have to get rid of to please God.

That is why this pandemic is taking place, not because of what is happening recently, but this is decades of disobedience that this world had shown to God. No reverence for God anymore, even in our music. I heard songs that had profanity mixed with God; God is a holy God; you cannot mix Him with filthy words and think that is ok with Him because it is not. We have to look at God as higher than us and respect Him and honor Him as our God and creator of all things.

So we got to do what God has called us to do; this is one reason I am pushing to write this book. We all need an increase in our faith, I included. We have to stop making excuses and start to trust God with our lives. We need to also trust him when we cannot trace him, sometimes God may not be speaking to you directly in some cases, but He is teaching you through experience that will make you better, stronger, and confident in God. I know He did that for me when I went through my 7-year torment. It made me so strong against the enemy that He did not know what hit him when I came out of what he put me through. So building through trials; it is not a bad thing; it is actually a good thing. The Bible says:

"As we know [with great confidence] that God [who is deeply concerned about us] caused all things to work together [as a plan] for good for those who love God, to those who are called according to His plan and purpose." Romans 8:28

We all have a purpose, but it is on the other side of our pain. That is why you have to praise God in the midst of your trial because it is only a trial, and you are coming out stronger than you went in. Look at building your faith as a blessing because as you build, you are getting closer to your destiny and purpose.

What God has truly designed for your life, don't you want to see that? I know I truly do, I know that number one God is important to me, and I want to please Him and also obtain everything that He has for me. Some people do not feel this way, but we all have a choice to make. You can either accept the mediocre of complaining about the issues or accept God's best, which the issues that you have can be opportunities to bless your life.

For example, if you are having issues with your children, there is an opportunity to pray on how to handle them differently. When you implement those strategies that God gives you, you start to see the changes right before your eyes; you may not see it right away but over time. God wants you to look at everything that you are going through as an opportunity to either bless you or bless someone else. This will build your faith so much when you do that. It will change your mindset and give you an optimistic outlook on life and God. That is how God wants you to look at everything in your life.

Chapter 10

Testify

T his chapter is a very unique chapter in this book. This chapter is a chapter that will give you great insight about my life and the lives of others. You will see 6 testimonies on how God loves and blesses His people. I was only going to let others tell theirs. But I wanted to share an untold testimony of my own. So you can see a detailed story about my life as well. Sometimes the writer can write about his/her own experiences, and the reader will feel that things like this only happens to the writer.

So that is why I decided to add this chapter to the book so you can see it in other people's lives and all the key tools that I have given you thus far in this book. Even though I am in it, I want you to dive in and experience other people's struggles and triumphs in their own lives. This chapter is a great way to believe that everything that the people in this chapter have gone through, the same things that they have overcame, are the same things you will overcome. So know that your affliction is just for a moment, and you will see victory after every storm that you face in your life. It is just the beginning of where God will take you and where you will go.

I am super excited about this chapter and all that you will experience, feel and relate to. Trust me, when you read these stories, you will laugh, cry and feel empowered to go forward in anything that you want to accomplish in your life. Things don't come easy but know as you move forward and take your faith journey, you will too experience great wins and will have a testimony just like all of these. I will start first, and then you will encounter so many beautiful real-life stories, so get ready for TESTIFY......

Title: From Sickness To Abundance
Testimony By: Shakeema S. Perry

Back in 2016, I was home and got really sick; I thought it was allergies because it felt the same way when I got it. I get allergies every year and get really sick because of it. Usually, it lasts maybe a few days, but this time; it lasted much longer. It was about a week. I was still going back and forth to work because I could not take any time off. So one day, I got really sick to the point I could barely get up. I wanted to go upstairs in my apartment to get something out of my room. When I was at the top of my steps, thank God I was not that close to the steps, but I was near the steps. Then I suddenly fell and passed out for about 30 seconds. I said to myself, something is not right with me; I need to go to the hospital.

I really should have called the ambulance, but I thought I was well enough to take myself. Once I got to the hospital, thank God

it was not crowded, and they took me in right away. I could
barely stand up; I was so fatigued. The doctor checked my vitals.
And my heart was fine. Then he checked my liver, and my
enzymes were way too high, which was not normal. I expected to
go in there and be in and out, but the doctor had to run more tests,
so they told me I had to be admitted. I was like, what, oh my
goodness, what is wrong with me. So when the doctors ran more
tests, they found that I had Hepatitis A.

I was like, what is that? I looked it up to get more information. I
was like, where did I get this from? This is so strange. So they told
me that they had to keep me for 2 days and ended up turning into
5 days. Those 5 days that I was in there was very difficult because
the symptoms of this virus were all over the place. One minute I
was cold, then I was hot. I had muscle pain, nausea, jaundice, and
other things that were going on for those days. I had some
wonderful people come to visit me. But I could not stand it, I
wanted to leave so bad. I had an I.V. in my arm the whole time I
was there, and I could barely wash up because it had to go with
me everywhere I went. I was so miserable; I asked God why is this
happening, because I did not fully understand it at all.

Then I felt a way because certain people did not come to see me.
The Lord told me, don't worry about who does not come or who
comes; I am here with you through this whole thing. God wanted
me to trust the process I was going through. So a health inspector
came in and asked me where I have dined in the last 30 days. I
gave her a few places, but tropical smoothie stood out, out of all of
them. So I did not think anything of it, so finally I was able to
leave the hospital. I was out of work for 2 more weeks. Which I
was happy about, I am not going to lie. I needed a break from all
the chaos at work being on the phones. Then come to find out

over 100 people was hospitalized because of Hepatitis A.

The reason is that tropical smoothie got some strawberries from Egypt that was contaminated with Hepatitis A. So I filed a class-action lawsuit against them, and in 2018 I received a 6 figure settlement. I paid off my hospital bills, credit cards, car note and even purchased a second car cash. I am not going to lie; that felt good, and I also sowed into my Church and others. You see, this story shows that all things work out for the good right, and that is how God will work in your life if you just trust Him.

Title: Through It All
Testimony By: Shalena Broaster

As I reflect upon rebuilding my life after a crushing break up, I marvel at my journey which began on June 18th, 2012. After being in a 6-year relationship that had grown toxic, I finally decided to leave. This was not an easy decision because my entire life was wrapped up in this relationship. I was engaged, living with my then fiancé and working for Him. We also had a beautiful son whom we both adored. Leaving was not an easy decision because I left behind everything I had come to know over the last 6 years: no more exotic vacations, easy living, a nice home, foreign cars, or a yacht.

When I left, I gave it all up for peace. I felt as if I lost myself in that relationship. I had gained weight, started losing my hair, and my body had become toxic. I also felt as if I gave up on my dreams of empowering women and building businesses using their God-given gifts and talents. During the weeks leading up to finally leaving, I realized that I had to empower myself first. I had to learn to love myself first before I could show others how to do so in full integrity. I was so bright-eyed and bushy-tailed when I first left. I was ready to conquer the world.

One of the major decisions I made when I left this relationship was to leave my son with his father as I tried to establish myself. You see, when I left, I became homeless. I needed to find housing, etc. I made it clear that it was my intention to come back to get my son when I got back on my feet. I missed him terribly. This spurred me to get myself together to come back for him. Getting back on my feet took longer than I thought it would. I was homeless for 2 years. I bounced from one family member's couch to another. Although I struggled, I did make progress on my dreams. The more I progressed, the more trouble began to brew between my ex and myself.

We would spend 3 years battling in family court over custody and child support. It seemed as though he would win every time. He ended up with primary physical custody, and I was ordered to pay him child support even though I didn't have a job. From 2013 to 2019, I went through bouts of depression. I would miss my son terribly. No one seemed to understand my pain. There were times I wanted to give up and end it all.

I would pray and ask God to deliver me from the hurt and pain. I must admit it took years because there were layers of pain and awareness. At the beginning of 2019, my stepmom died of cancer. Before she passed, she told me that God wanted to use my mind, but He couldn't because I needed to let some things go. She was right; my mind was preoccupied with the past and my pain. After she passed, I dedicated myself to learning how to trust God again and love myself. By the time 2020 arrived, I was a new woman.

Not only did I get married during the pandemic, but God also began to use me mightily in my business. I made 6 figures in a few months. The best part was being able to touch the lives of so many women who invested in my coaching.

Always remember that God will never leave you nor forsake you. Whether you are at rock bottom or at the mountain top, He is always there for you. There's nothing you can't recover from. There's nothing you can't achieve with God guiding you. You can create the life you dream of. God cares about the total woman. He wants you to prosper in all areas of your life.

Title: Fearless
Testimony by: Rudyard Stephens

I was born in Westmoreland, Jamaica, to a single mom and was raised with God-fearing grandparents. So I was introduced to God at a very young age, but I became very difficult to handle, and my mom felt overwhelmed and not knowing what else to do. She gave me up to foster care at age 13. A woman adopted me, and I lived with my foster mom, and she loved God as well, and she took me to Church, but I was still a lost young man, although I had known God since I could comprehend and believed that Jesus died for my sins. I had never been overtaken by the flood of the Holy Spirit, and in my mind, I started to have doubts. The doubts led to inconsistencies in my behavior. Some years, I would do really well, then other years not so well.

I ruined my chance at college scholarships, and unsure what I would do next, I joined the U.S Navy. Finally, I was out on my own and able to make my own decisions. I would love to say that I was disciplined and remembered the lesson of my childhood. How I was taught to lean on God for direction and purpose in my life went out of the window. My mind had been trained to respond differently.

As the seeds fell among the thorns, they were choked out. I laid aside my childhood lessons where I witnessed faith and prayer as tools of success. Instead, I chose to seek after the treasures of this world. I could write books upon books about the unrighteous paths my life took for the next four years. I was so carried away in my selfishness that I distanced myself from my family because I did not want to hear about God. Eventually, my reckless, faithless, unguided lifestyle caught up with me. I was convicted of a serious crime and dishonorably discharged from the Navy.

After pleading guilty, my sentence was reduced from five years to a few months. Life after incarceration was tough. I was on probation, which I couldn't handle. My service had put me in Norfolk, Virginia, where the only people I knew were sailors who served with me. But after my arrest and incarceration, they really didn't want anything to do with me. Because of my probation, I was not able to leave Norfolk. So I was left with nothing and no one. I gained a place to live, a job, and even enrolled in school. But that was not enough to defeat the evil habits that I had allowed to overtake my mind.

Within less than a year's time, I was prosecuted twice, and the second time I brought back a second charge even more serious than the first and carried over ten years. I was given four years for the new charge, and at my probation violation hearing, I was given all 5 years back, and my time was set to run consecutively. This meant that I would do the four years first, and then I would do the five years. Back in my jail pod that night, I cried, begged God to save me, asked God why, and grieved over how I would do nine years in prison, but I got no answer. So I cursed God and refused to believe He even existed.

My first two years in prison were very hard. The constant loneliness, fear, lack of freedom, and being reminded four to five times a day that you are not in control of anything in your life was unbearable. Some nights, the emotional pain would be so hard that I wanted to die. Not by suicide, but I desired to just fade away, to not exist, and I refused to hold myself responsible. I would talk about the unfairness of the system and justify my crime by saying things like, "The crime was not that bad," "no one was hurt," and "it's too much time."

 And I would blame the same God that at the same time I was saying did not exist. This led me to join an atheist group in prison that taught that God, as I knew it, was a white man's creation to enslave the black man and that I was God. In this atheist group, I was given all kinds of "knowledge" to study, including the Bible, and I did it studiously. I exhibited a level of discipline and dedication that I did not even know I was capable of. I had been following this lifestyle for a little over three years. But no matter how much knowledge I gained, it all seemed to be missing something. I found myself referring to the Bible in conversations and "building sessions," as we called it. I asked questions that my brothers could not clearly explain. They told me it was lies. But consciousness began to awaken me every time I referred to myself as being the Supreme Being, and nothing was greater than I.

One day while I was in my cell by myself, I was reading a book about the universe and how it operates. And for the first time, I heard God's voice. He said, "I am the only one that can do that, and I am the only one that can help you." At that moment, all the lessons from my childhood and the examples I had seen pop back in my mind, the scriptures I had read and memorized and could not make to mean anything other than what it said, rang as truth, and it was as if my spirit let out a yell of triumph, screaming, "Finally!!!" Because to my core, I knew without a shadow of a doubt that God was real, Jesus was real, and that He was the Son of God and that He died on the cross for my sins. The next day, I stayed in my cell and avoided my "brothers" because I could not continue in the lie that I had been living for the last three years.

I spent the day praying and reading my Bible, asking God for guidance on what to do next. But actually, God did not have to tell me what to do next; I knew what I had to do next. I had no fear of doing it, but my pride was the demon that I had to stomp down in order to do it. The following day at the building session, I stood before nine of my "brothers" and told them that I believed Jesus was the Son of God and that He died for my sins. I told them that I accept His death as my salvation, and now I am free.

After my pronouncement, my hunger for the Word of God grew tremendously. I couldn't get enough. I read the Word everywhere and at all times. I lost interest in the things that were worldly on T.V, shows like explicit music. All I was watching was J.C T.V and the WORD network because we had those channels in prison. They were the only place I could get more of God. I did not go to the church services because too many other things went on there. So, I had Church in my cell by myself and watched whatever T.V ministry was on. I longed to get out and find a church home of my own.

After 8 1/2 years, I was released from prison here to Richmond, Virginia, another place where I had nothing and no one. But this time, I had Jesus. In my last years of being locked up, the Lord helped me to map out goals, dreams, and purpose for my life. He told me to hold fast to Zephaniah 3:19,

"At that time, I will deal with all who oppressed you. I will rescue the lame; I will gather the exiles. I will give them praise and honor in every land where they have suffered shame."

Because He knew how ashamed I had been and that I was unsure of how I could make it back, He gave me hope.

He asked me to be faithful in my walk with Him, and He would do the rest. The road has been rough, and every time I felt like I would falter, God gave me the strength to carry through. That's why I stand before you today, seven years free. Through the grace of God, I am married to my beautiful wife who fears God, father to a healthy baby girl, within a career with advancement opportunities, working towards entrepreneurship, and a member of an impactful church. I have so much further to go because I am called to God's purpose, and I look forward to where He will take me.

Title: God's Promises
Testimony by: Casey Alexis

Allow me to testify about the promises of God and His faithfulness to those of us who believe. By faith, God promises in His Word,

"Ask and it will be given to you; seek and you will find; knock and the door will be opened to you. For everyone who asks receives; the one who seeks finds; and to the one who knocks, the door will be opened." (Matthew 7:7-8)

When my husband and I got married in 2006, we were young and excited about all we hoped for in life. Like any young couple, we had dreams of what we thought our lives would be once we got married. We were grown now, and with being grown, we were ready to do grown people things, LOL. A year into our marriage, we found out we were expecting. We were shocked, excited, and filled with joy about the gift of life we were blessed enough to conceive. I scheduled our first prenatal appointment, and we headed into the Dr.'s office with excitement!

As I laid down for the examination, a nurse came into the room with the fetal heart monitor so she could find the baby's heartbeat. Unfortunately, she had no success but reassured us how this happens all the time, so we got an ultrasound. Naturally, I became a bit nervous and began to feel anxious. My husband grabs my hand, and we silently looked at each other in fear of the worst. So, we get to the ultrasound room, and the tech begins the examination. She looks around, but she is eerily silent. I began to realize something isn't right. She shows us the baby, but there isn't any movement.

The tech hints that usually around this time, eight weeks to be exact, there should be some movement. There wasn't any, so the physician comes into the room and explains that we had experienced a miscarriage. Our baby had stopped growing, and there was nothing we could do but wait for my body to do what was expected or undergo a procedure.

I will never forget the feeling as we got into the car in complete silence, I buckled up my seatbelt, and I began to cry. My husband tried to console me, but I was inconsolable. I never held this child nor felt its breath, but that was still my baby. When we got married, the dreams we had did not include any of this, I cried out to God in agony, trying to understand what went wrong. Unfortunately, the scene at the Dr.'s office that day did not happen to us that one time.

In fact, in the following 4 years of our marriage, it happened two more times. We experienced a total of three miscarriages, and we could not understand why this continued to happen to us.

With those three occurrences, I continued to opt-out of the procedure, I allowed my body to do what it naturally was called to do, and with each time, I gave birth to death. After the third time, I felt defeated as a woman, as a wife, and as a child of God. To stay afloat and not lose hope, I would have my husband read me Hannah's story in 1 Samuel. Each time I would cry out to the Lord in anguish. Praying that the story of Hannah would be real in my life. As we continued to read the story, I began to realize that Hannah never stopped pleading before God until He answered her prayers.

She never resolved to not having children; she kept believing and trusting in God for a miracle, she had faith. I also began to read the stories of other women in the Bible who could not conceive, but God came through even when it seemed physically impossible for them to have children. I held onto the promises of God and began to seek Him, knock, and ask Him why. Why is this happening to us when His Word declared us to be fruitful and to multiply? How could we be children of God and not be able to do what Our Father declared?

I resolved within myself, like Hannah, to hold onto God's Word. God is not a man that He should lie. Therefore, His promises are true, and they are yes and amen. The more I held onto His Word, the more my faith began to grow; the more it grew, the more I believed. I refused to believe that I was unable to give birth to a living child. God said it, so shall it be in my life. I took my faith into action and began to fast and pray, seeking His face for the door opened in our lives that was causing these miscarriages. I sought answers, and as promised, He revealed the truth behind the miscarriages.

Once the truth was revealed, my husband and I were able to close that door shut and seal it by the power of the blood of Jesus Christ. From then on, we were able to receive the blessing of the fruit of the womb. On November 25th, 2011, we welcomed our first living child; two and a half years later, our second daughter was born. As I testify of God's goodness, I am presently five months pregnant with our son. My testimony is valid, God's promises are true, what He has done for me, He can do for you. Trust Him, have faith, and believe.

Title: It Was Good That I Was Afflicted
Testimony by: Amy Venable-Turner

It was good when I was afflicted when the Pastor fired me as the Chief Operating Officer and the head of the organization. To add further insult to injury, he asked that the authorities be present to escort me off the premises in the event I did not react well to the news. Although I would never behave that way, he knew how much I had sacrificed over those five years and how I walked away from my own business to assist their organization. He knew I was extremely dedicated and committed to the organization, so getting terminated without any wrongdoing would come as a total shock. Needless to say, it was, in fact a total shock! "God, where are you?" "I don't understand!" "What am I supposed to do now? "

These were a few of the questions swirling around as I lay on the couch for two weeks and moped. God was getting ready to teach me the weight of that scripture found over in Psalm 119:71

"It was good that I was afflicted so that I might learn your decrees."

I never really understood the weight or the meaning of this scripture until this moment. Who would ever embrace trouble, humiliation, injustice? I kind of skipped over those scriptures like "Count it all Joy" James 1:2 and "Glory in tribulation" Romans 5:3. They made no natural sense to me. However, I know that pain has a way of teaching you lessons that you will never learn any other way. Two weeks after my humiliating termination, my phone rang. It was the director of the childcare center that I owned.

While I worked for the other organization, I still held on to the childcare center to understand that I would return when my assignment was complete. She had done such an excellent job in my absence that my integrity would not let me fire her because I no longer had a job. There simply was not enough in the budget for the both of us; it was just an impossible situation. Thanks be to God, who always gives us the victory; we serve a God who specializes in impossible situations.

She said, "Ms. Venable, are you dressed?" I reluctantly answered her but quickly responded, "Why?" "She said there is someone who would like to meet you." She explained there was a nearby daycare that was closing, and they were going to place all of their children in our center, but they just wanted to meet the owner! I jumped up off the sofa in total disbelief! You see, this meant that there would suddenly now be enough money to support both our salaries! Just like that, God moved! In an instant, my tears dried up! I knew this was a divine set up! I knew God put our childcare center in the heart of that woman!

There were so many children that we ended up taking over their location. We opened up a 3rd location, and I became known as the lady who takes over daycares! My salary tripled. We are now working on our 4th location and expanding to take over commercial strip malls. That affliction birthed out millions instead of thousands.

That affliction got me to see God on a whole other level! That affliction shifted my entire life and lifestyle! If you can go through and keep the proper attitude while you are going through. God will vindicate you! He will establish you, and you will come out greater on the other side! Just know that trouble is simply an indicator that promotion is at hand. So rejoice and be confident that it truly is going to work for your good! For He knows the way, He is taking us!

Title: The 24th Hour Miracle
Testimony by: Isaiah Little

August 24th, 2020 was the day my life took an unexpected turn. I am a husband, father of 3 children, a musical and staff worship leader for a well-known church organization. I mention these to give a little context to my main focus daily. On August 20th, 2020, I woke up to an uncomfortable pain in my arm, which I brushed off as a possible cramp from sleeping on it the wrong way. To my surprise, what I assumed would correct itself maybe after a day turned into a consistent annoyance for three days. Determined to manage all the many things I needed to, I continued to assume the best that it would soon subside and I'd be back to my normal self in no time.

What I discovered on August 24th was that it was not an issue that I should have pushed off so nonchalantly. I brought my 5-

year-old son to work with me that morning to assist him with his kindergarten online work for the day. Everything seemed to be going well until we reached his lunch break. That is when the once annoying pain from my arm had transitioned to my chest. I took him to grab his lunch and stumbled out of the car upon arriving at our food destination. I can't even begin to express what was so intense at that moment and what was happening to my body. But as quick as it happened, it was somehow interrupted by my right pinky finger being slammed in our car door. Which jolted me back and left me stunned and just feeling confused about what had just taken place.

After returning to work, I asked one of my co-workers to drive me to the nearest urgent care, and from there, we were in the hospital. Where cardiologist ran a test on me and soon explained that I had suffered a mild heart attack. 35 years old, you can only imagine the cold uncomforted feeling that washed over me after hearing those words. The miracle was that there was no damage to my heart or any of my organs; I came out of it untouched by what should have ultimately taken me out. Although the mental and spiritual battle to proceed after such a victory was not expected. I couldn't find peace in the "Miracle" I needed closure from God, an explanation as to why this had happened to me.

I fell into a deep depression for several weeks and couldn't shake it as hard as I tried. I sought out professional help, solicited prayer, and all the support I could get from family and friends. But what I realized was God was missing from the equation. I needed to place my trust in the one who manufactured my heart in the first place and acknowledge Him in the storm I was facing. I began to get up early in the morning and pray and read my Bible, go over old sermons that my Pastor preached.

I was fearful, afraid to live; I felt fragile and broken. But through inviting God into my pain and brokenness, I was able to regain the strength and focus I felt I lost. I was able to hope again and trust in God like never before. Because I remembered who I am and who's I am, I was able to overcome. There are still small struggles I do deal with, but the difference is, I don't deal with it alone; I've invited Jesus into the storm to guide me through.

Wow! All of these testimonies that you read had me in tears. This was not fake news, these are real people with real-life issues that served God and trusted him through the process, and that is why they overcame every trial. I hope that these powerful testimonies encouraged you and encouraged your walk with God to keep on going and trusting God for everything. Yes, it is tough out there, but you don't have to walk this journey alone. God loves you, and He cares so much about you, and He wants you to know that He does not have any respect of person. That means the same that He did for someone else is the same thing He can do for you.

Knowing that all the Lord wants is you to trust Him for your life because He knows the way you should take. He wants to make sure that you get to your destination. He knows all, so that is why He requires us to trust Him. Don't you want to follow an all-knowing God? I know I do because there is no wrong way in Him leading and guiding me when I do. I will always have access to greatness because He is with me. He is also with you, so be encouraged to make it through any trial that you are going through in your life.

Chapter 11

Fight for your Faith

Every day you have to fight for what is already yours. I know that sounds a little strange, but what I mean is, even though it is yours does not mean that the enemy will not fight against you to get what God has for you, and one of them is your faith. Doubt always wants to take over your faith, and you cannot let it. Your faith in God has to be strong, and you should have faith in your abilities that God has given you. The enemy wants to snatch the faith you have in God and in yourself because once that is taken away, worry, doubt, and insecurity seeps in your mind and heart.

That would put your faith on pause or permanently stopped, because now you have nothing to stand on to go after your purpose and destiny. You need your faith in order to do that, because your faith actually activates your progress on what you go after and strive for. Without faith, you will not think it is worth going after or putting in your time to make your dream a reality. It is easier to fight for your faith when you are connected to the right people.

That is why the Bible wants us to gather in His temple in Hebrews

10:25.

"It says not forsaking the assembling of ourselves together as the manner of some is, but exhorting one another and so much the more, as ye see the day approaching."

God wants us to come together in our faith to build each other up. Some people like to tear each other down. I am not saying all church folks have that mindset, but they are others that think the way you do.

Connect to them and that will help you with your faith fight because there is always life spoken into you. You are who you are around, some of you don't believe that you may not see it right away, but the longer, or how much time you are with someone that is negative or positive, that is who you become. But that is your choice who you want to be around, but I would suggest positive people as much as possible.

It is like you say that you don't drink alcohol, but you hang out with someone that always drink and always drinks around you. Eventually you will start drinking, that is human nature. Our flesh is always weak based on what we feed it on a daily basis. If you constantly pray and spend time with God and His word and be around positive people to grow in maturity in Christ.

In most cases, you will become the environment that you are in. I tend to stay around a lot of positive people that love me, encourage me, and tell the truth about me, that are truly happy for me because you need those type of friends to tell you when you are wrong. This kept me in the right state of mind concerning my future. I have wonderful Pastors & Spiritual Parents who always preach faith, which helps me believe in God even more and stay focused on what God wants me to do.

If you have that in your life, your spirit will grow strong, and also your belief system will go to the next level. That is what is going to keep you through the process when times get rough and your faith is pretty low, because negative is all around you that is why you need prayer, God's Word, positive people, faith-based Pastors to keep you strong in your faith. So, that is how you fight and choose faith over fear every time. So my question to you is what do you prefer? In life you have to make choices and decisions in how you get to your destination that God designed for you.

God will not force you to do something you don't want to do, but He will tug at your heart, speak to you and try to guide you down the right path to success that He has you on, but remember you have to answer to God in what you did not do one day. So I would admonish you to listen to God and do it His way, because it is the best way I know, because He has not steer me in the wrong direction yet.

Don't give up because it gets too hard, hard is actually a strength that you will need for your next level that you will go to. But if you will let hard stop you, you will never see or experience your next level. Your next level can be the next level of the desires of your heart. Something you always wanted and dreamed of. So you have to keep on fighting for each level to get to the next level. If anyone told you that faith was easy then they have mislead you, because it is not. When you decide that faith will stay in your life no matter what. You will face heartache, pain, disappointments, setbacks, failure, etc. You will get through all of this because of the faith that you decided to keep even though you endured all of these things in your life.

Also, how can you use the faith that you have without all of these things happening in your life? How can you be built up in faith if these things have not entered your life? That is when you truly know that you have faith; when things try to fight against it.

This is the only way to win in your life. If you don't use what you have, which is your faith that God has given you, then you will feel defeated every time opposition comes your way. Even though you are not defeated, but your perception is telling you that you are. Then eventually you will lose your faith, because you feel that you don't have it. You will start to get to a place where you give up. Faith helps you to get to your win, when you have seen so many losses in your life. So hold on to your faith for dear life because you will need it to conquer the battles you need to face.

Also, always embed this principle in your children because they will need it to survive as well. One thing I know that my dad has always embedded in me was to have faith in God no matter what, not only did he tell me that, but he was an example of what faith truly looked like. He did not have that true example in his life growing up, but he went to church and heard a sermon that changed his life. When he knew that he can have anything he wanted with hard work and moving by faith, he was able to grow a successful business for over 30 years.

He has a few homes, multiple cars and a Yacht. He has cars that are over hundreds of thousands of dollars, because of his faith. My dad is from Bedford-Stuyvesant do or die Brooklyn, N.Y; that is what people call it, which is one of the toughest places in Brooklyn. He was poor and he and his siblings did not have much growing up, but he had God and determination that he wanted a better life for him and his family. He fought for his faith.

Are you going to do the same? Having faith in something that you desire, does not automatically put a silver spoon in your mouth. It is a process that you have to go through to get to your win on the other side of your faith. There is always a win if you don't give up and lose your faith. Also, know that your faith is worth fighting for. It is worth every pain, tear, loss, fear. It is all worth it. Look at faith as a lifeline to your dreams and purpose. If you don't push through, you are not going to survive. That is how you have to view it and how important it has to be. So that is how you fight for your faith.

Chapter 12

Your Faith will Carry You

Look at your faith as transportation. I will use a car for an example, so for you to get from point A to point B, you have to do what first? You have to take your key and put it in the ignition, turn the car on, check your rearview, put your foot on the brake, shift gears and then put your foot on the gas and then drive to your destination. Do you see all the components of your faith?

It was a step by step process to get to your destination. So that is how faith works; you have to do some things and put them into action to see the blessed outcome. It is not that simple as a car, but it was an example of the process that faith takes for it to work in your life. Your faith will carry you if you let it; it has the power to get you through the hardest moments in your life.

So when you back up action in what you are believing God for. You will see things start to move in your life because you did not just look at faith as a word, but you looked at faith as an action word that you had to move on in order to see the vision that you dreamed of before it happened. It is just like me writing this book; it was a process. I got the idea of the title from God, then I started writing in a notebook, which was my draft copy, then I typed it out which is my manuscript.

Then it has to go to editing, page design, book cover, and then publishing. If I skipped any of these steps, then you will not be holding this book in your hands and reading it right now. This is what faith is. Everything in life is a process and steps in order to achieve what you want to accomplish. Nothing just automatically comes to you, that is not how it works.

If you do think that it works that way, get that thought process out of your mind. It is not true; if you don't walk by faith, you will never get to where you want to be in your life, your dreams, and what you are capable of. You will never see the prophecies that were spoken over your life years ago come to pass. You are definitely capable of doing great things, but you have to know that it takes action in order to achieve it. Challenges that you face often shows you what is on the inside of you that you never saw before.

I never thought in a million years that I would be an author of any book, but here I am writing my second book, isn't that amazing? You can do precisely the same if you desire, but your perception of faith has to change in order for you to be all that God has called you to be. You have to look at faith as I can't see it, but I believe, and with my part that I play in this along with my faith, I will start to see things work in my favor.

Your part is very significant when it comes to your faith. You cannot have faith without your works that you bring to the table, because that is not faith if you don't take action. Your action is the function of your faith; you cannot have one without the other. So action plays a major part of you seeing your faith working for you. I am glad that God designed it that way, because if everything was so simple and easy, we would not appreciate what God has given us.

You may say I would appreciate it, no you will not look at Adam & Eve they had everything given to them, and just with their disobedience, they lost everything just like that. Some of you would probably say if I was Adam or Eve, I would not have done that, but that is wrong again. It is human nature that man is never satisfied, especially when something is just handed to them without work.

I would make an example of my house, when I tried to purchase my house, it was not an easy process and I almost did not get this house because the seller had to drop the price in order to sell it to me. So because it was such a fight, I appreciate this house much more than I would have if it was given to me so freely. That is how we are, and if you deny that just watch when someone gives you something without a price and see how you treat it based on something that you spent your hard earn money buying it will definitely be a difference.

Sometimes God allows the struggle because it helps you to value what He has given you. Sometimes we complain too much and God has given us enough in our hands to accomplish every dream that we want to go after. But we want to blame someone else or make excuses of why we cannot get it done. We have to stop doing that because our complaints do not change our circumstances at all. It just wastes time that you can use to bring your dreams alive in your life. You can make it happen; everything you need to get what you want is inside of you. You just have to tap into your God-given gifts and talents and start to use them one by one.

You don't have to start with multiple things, just start with one, maximize on that talent, and then move on to the next. If you simplify it, it will not be so overwhelming. I remember one time in my life, I was trying to accomplish multiple things while working a full-time job. I became so overwhelmed that I stopped doing anything concerning all that I was doing. You don't want that, so work on one thing at a time and grow from that. So what I mean is work on one of the gifts you enjoy doing and research that gift or field you want to go into and see what it will take to start it up.

If you can find a coach or mentor to teach you and guide you through the process, you may have to pay them, but it will all be worth it because you will feel more at ease. That is what I did, I am a Coach, and I also have a Coach, and it does not make me feel less of a person, it actually let me know that I do not know it all, and that is okay. None of us know it all; there is always something that we can learn in life. With me having a Coach, I made thousands of dollars in my Coaching business because I listened and followed my coach's instructions, which is why I am successful.

Sometimes you have to get out of your own way and humble yourself and listen; we do not know everything because if we did, then we would not need God. Even though some of us think we don't but let tragedy strike, they will call on God because now they need Him. But it is self-evident that we do base on all the chaos in the world today. Only God can fix these issues that we are dealing with. You know how He will resolve these issues by making Himself known and changing the heart of men toward Him.

Unfortunately, we at most times come to know God during challenging times. This is because people do not recognize God until their whole world is shaken by the foundation. Then some of us tend to hear God much clearer in this position. Sometimes it is not a tragedy, but sometimes it can be an impact in your life for you to understand what God is saying.

One way that God had to open up our eyes was 9/11 when N.Y was rocked like never before with the World Trade Center getting hit by two planes. We did not expect that these two tall buildings will fall down the way they did. Thousands of people perished that day. Did it get our attention? Yes, some of us drew closer to God because of it. Churches were filled and did not have any room on some Sundays.

But nowadays, people begin to forget God again until tragedy strikes. Like this current pandemic, now people want to pray and go to church because all they have is their faith in God. I'm not saying that God creates the tragedies, but He allows it to get us in the right position in our hearts to change towards Him. This is a known pattern for us as humans; we only move when fire is up our behinds. It is true, but I don't want fire, I just want to obey and do what God wants me to do in this life before heaven, and you should want the same thing.

Man has a choice and a decision to do good or evil, so many times, it is us that brings tragedy in our lives. But sometimes, God allows tragedy to strike to get our full attention. It works every time but does it last long in most cases? No, but you do get a hand full of people that finally get what God is trying to do in their lives. That is why it is good to serve God and keep your faith and trust in Him. So when it comes to your life being impacted to get your attention, it could be a car accident that almost took your life, and God speared your life; it could be you almost drowning doing a water stunt with friends. It could be anything that God uses to get your attention. For me, it was God allowing me not to hear out of my left ear for two weeks that definitely got my attention, and I have not turned back ever since.

The whole point of this is that God wants us to be humble to receive blessings by faith. You can have that faith for something and go after it, and it does not happen because we are not ready for it, because some of us think we are better than everyone else; that is not humility. God wants us to receive so we can give back to others. But if we are conceded, we will be selfish and won't want to help anybody but ourselves. That is not the heart of God, so that is why our trials of life are so necessary to our growth.

We all need to grow, and we all need our faith to get us there. That is why I say our faith carries us. When we allow our faith to get us to our destination, in turn, we grow, we get stronger, we learn lessons, and we appreciate our life and journey. We understand other people that were in our shoes. It is so much to obtain that is good in our lives through our faith. Faith is very imperative to our success.

Chapter 13
Have Faith in Yourself

Having faith in yourself means that you have faith in your abilities, gifts, and talents that God has given you. By doing this, when obstacles come that may be too big for you or you afraid to do, you have to look on the inside of yourself and believe that you can accomplish anything that you put your mind to. Once you believe that you can do it, then you ask God to build your faith in Him for the journey of you taking this leap of faith. You believing that you can do it is the first step, and the journey of getting there is your faith in God because you cannot do it alone and walk in peace without God.

Only believing in yourself will start to fade with opposition that will take place in your life. But having faith in yourself and God gives you ammunition to succeed; without doubt, you and God together are unstoppable. Some people only have faith in themselves but have a harder journey without God. But with God, you will have the peace that surpasses all understanding while you are going through your process to the promise of the dream you want to accomplish.

So that is the difference with someone with God and someone

without God. Peace will be the missing link. Wouldn't you want to have God's peace as you work and wait on the Lord? I know that I do and I am experiencing that peace actually as I am writing this book for you and I. Writing this book is allowing me to know that I am using my God-given abilities to get this book into all of your hands by doing my part in making it happen because I believe in myself that I can make this happen.

That is why it is super essential to believe in yourself. But one thing that you don't want to do is to believe in yourself so much that you think you don't need God. This is really dangerous because as soon as you say that you don't need God in your heart, you will have difficulty getting to the other side of your dream and purpose. So I would suggest that you include God in every area of your life.

Do you know when you tap into your God-given abilities and your faith in God, you tap into the unlimited? There is no limit to where you can be or where you could go. Most times, we say we believe God can do it, but we sit on our gifts and lack faith in our own abilities to get whatever needs to be done in our lives. So we have to have both, which is the belief in ourselves and God all at the same time to be consistently successful.

You may ask what I mean by consistent success. What I mean is having a constant flow of success. Every time you turn around, success follows you everywhere you go. It is like an explosive that keeps going off. This type of success does not happen overnight; it takes time to grow and you have to put a lot of effort into working on it. Either if it is a dream or a goal that you are working towards. That is how you build yourself to get there, but you have to be very consistent in what you are doing to see that type of flow in your life.

I want you to know that it is not only possible for you to survive but to thrive in life, but you must believe in yourself first then in your creator God. Then go after everything you believe in with all of your might. You will see God move in miraculous ways, and it will blow your mind. You may not see it right away, and it will take some time, or in some cases, you may not see everything that you desire, sometimes it will happen for your children or children's children.

In the Bible, David was originally supposed to build a temple for God, but because David was a warrior and shed blood, instead Solomon his son took on building the temple for God. So what I mean regarding this scripture in the Bible is that God has so much in store for you and your future, and it is so massive that it is passed down to your offspring. The reason is that your blessings may outlive you, that is how big it is.

God has not forgotten about you, you just have to do your part and be patient and you will start to see the things that God has told you that will manifest in your life. God can't lie; He will do what He said He will do it every time. He is a God that keeps His promises. He loves His people profoundly, and he wants us to thrive on this earth according to His will for your life.

We must seek the will of God for our daily lives, then we will start to see our gifts and abilities that God has given us, and you have to believe that you can do it. Then you ask God to empower you to complete the task and go through the process, but God needs you to have faith in yourself as well as Him because He has created you, and He wants to connect to His creation, which is within yourself in a way that is pleasing to Him. Not pompous or arrogant, but to love and believe that He has given you everything you need to be equipped for your assignment on this earth.

So believe that you can achieve everything that your heart desires. God has you, and you have to know that with all of you. Do not doubt the gifts and talents that God has given you because everything that He created is good. Sometimes I believe that we doubt because we sometimes compare, compete and care. Let's start with the word compare; we have such a habit of comparing ourselves to others.

When we do this, we think that someone's gift is more significant than our own gifts, which is not actually true. God has given us individual gifts for a reason. We are all a piece and a part of this world so it can operate correctly. Everyone cannot be doctors, then how are they going to survive without nurses to assist.

Our purpose is supposed to assist one another and help each other grow, not to tear each other down with our mouths and what we say. We also compare to downplay someone else gifts to make our gift significant then someone else. That is not right either, and that comes from insecurity in both ways, thinking someone is better than you and thinking you better than someone else. I know that you won't want to admit that if this is you. But the truth will set you free today. You don't have to compare yourself to no one; you are fearfully and wonderfully made. Just concentrate on what your gifts are and use them to the best of your ability.

Also, when someone is very successful, we tend to only see from the outside, and we don't know the internal struggle of what that other person on how they fought and how they felt to get where they are, especially when they are on a different level then we are. Everyone who wants to win and does not have a wealthy background must start from the bottom and work their way up.

There are no handouts when it comes to being successful. I am not saying that you cannot get help, but what I am saying that you have to put in the majority of the work to make your success happen in your life. So when we see somebody on the top, celebrate them and be inspired, because you only see the victory in their life you never saw those times when they have felt defeated and decided to keep going. That is what you have to do every day in your life if you want to win.

So we need to stop comparing our gifts and abilities to someone else. We have to walk in our own path to success and how God desires for us to be. He made us unique for a reason. So walk in it and embrace every gift that God has given you and maximize the strong abilities you have now until more is revealed. All of us have not discovered all of our gifts and talents. I did not know I was a good writer until I wrote my first book, and someone told me that I was. Don't compare yourself to no one, because you are confident in your own gifts, so shine, baby, shine.

Now let us look at the word 'compete.' Now, this can get very ugly if you let it. I believe in friendly competition, but there is a thin line, and you have to make sure that you don't get so serious that now you don't even like the person anymore and want to see them lose and under you. When you start to get that serious and not friendly, you are no longer in friendly competition; you are in a place where you will lose every time.

When you compete with someone on your level or higher, you end up losing in the end. Either you will lose the competition because they are beating you so bad or winning, and you are putting too much pressure and anxiety on yourself and you are definitely not at peace. You will be always checking for them before you move, and that is no way to live. Also, competition does not care who it hurts, who you have to step on to get there.

Competition is also another form of insecurity. That is when you are so insecure with your gifts that you start to compete in an area that is no longer operating in your gifts, but now you are operating in someone else's God-given gift. When you do this, you already lose before you started because you are graced in your abilities, not other people's abilities. You will lose every time you do that, because it is not God's will for you to compete to make yourself better than someone else.

God wants you to love and embrace the gifts that He has given you and walk in them with confidence without apology. So when you do that, you are unstoppable, no one can't compete with you, and no one can do it like you. This is how you are supposed to be when it comes to you and your gifts. That is why this is so imperative that you love and guard your gifts. It is precious to God because He has given it to you for you to take territory and give Him all the glory in the process.

The last one is care. You may ask yourself the question, why did I used the word care. This is an important one then all the C's because, in life, we tend to care about almost anyone's reaction toward us, how they view us, and their opinion about us. When you are gifted by God, we should not care what other people think, when it comes to operating in our gifts. I am not saying you shouldn't care about people; I am saying do not care about people's opinions about what you are doing to walk in God's purpose. Now, if someone is giving you sound wisdom to help you, that is fine, but downplaying your gifts and who you are shouldn't be allowed.

Usually, in most cases, they are dealing with an internal struggle that has nothing to do with you. They want you to feel guilty that you are walking in God's purpose. They want to get under your skin and get you mad, so you will get distracted and not do what you are called or purposed to do. As a Christian, you just have to pray for them that they will walk in their own God-given gifts so they won't mess with you or anyone else to stifle them on their journey.

We all have a journey to walk, either it is God's plans or our own plans. But I would choose God's plans any day of the week. The Bible says that we all have our own cross to bear. So take up your cross and walk the path that God has given you and remember that path will lead you to success in every area of your life.

Chapter 14

Faith Over Fear

How do you win over your fears? First in order to conquer it, you must first study it. Why study it? Because when you want to take something or someone down, you have to study your opponent. Let's define fear; fear means an unpleasant emotion caused by the belief that someone or something is dangerous, likely to cause pain or a threat. So let's take a look at the first sentence. The first word that sticks out to me is emotion. So fear broken down has emotion in it, interesting. As people, are we able to control our emotions? I would say yes, not saying that you would not feel emotion; I am saying that we should know how to control them. We cannot let our emotions control us; we have to control them.

The next word that sticks out to me is the belief, so what you believe determines your emotions. If something terrible will happen that will trigger fear, you should counter it by believing something good will happen that will triggers faith. Our belief system is crucial and vital to our lives because it determines how we feel about a situation. So, you have to start believing the best outcome and not the worse one. This will trigger your emotions in the right direction so you can start to walk by faith over fear. The Bible says, in Proverbs 23:7

"For as he thinks in his heart so is he. So whatever you believe you will become."

The last word I want you to look at is pain; I know many of us do not like that word, including myself. As humans, we dislike pain because this is something that we don't like to feel, we run from it. But what if I told you that pain is what is going to get you to the other side of your millions. Would you go through it? Pain actually births resilience; it also builds compassion. It is what is needed to get you to your destination. We all have to go through it at some point in our lives either we go through it when we turn our back on the process or go through the process with God. I rather go through the process to get what is on the other side then go through the pain in lack and no destiny and purpose. Either way, pain is necessary.

Now, what does this have to do with fear? Remember that you have to study your opponent; you just did. If we controlled our emotions, believing the right things, and knowing that pain is part of our process, then where is fear when we do these things. Fear is now non-existent in our lives. Fear is only relevant if we make it to be. We are actually afraid of nothing that may never happen. Does that make more sense? We have the power to bind and loose, we bind fear, and we lose blessings in our lives. We have to do our part, and fear will no longer have power over you.

We have nothing to be afraid of, you may have a question on how to change your belief system, and one way is to stop watching everything on TV that has nothing to do with your future and where you are going. You need to start watching the right things to stimulate your mind for growth. Like inspiration programs that will inspire you, anything positive that doesn't put you in a negative state. Stay away from scary movies, I know some of you are probably sighing right now, but I am only helping you. If you know it or not, scary film will get into your psyche and mess you all up internally in your subconscious, so it is no good for you.

What you listen to is very important, listen to motivational messages that will motivate you to strive for better and be better as much as you can, at least 3 to 4 times a week, and if you have to, it can be daily. This will help you change your belief system.

Here are some examples of people you can listen to, Devon Franklin, Trent Shelton, Lisa Nichols, Eric Thomas, etc. They also have books you can purchase to help you. As you implement this, you will start to see that fear go away, but you have to be consistent in order to see that type of result. It is important you surround yourself with the right people who are encouraging you instead of discouraging you; this will help build your confidence in who you are and what God has called you to be.

 You don't want to doubt the things that God has told you being around the wrong people. Trust in God by reading His Word; the reason why I say this is because when you believe in God, there is nothing unreachable for you. There is no place that you cannot go if God permits you to be there. The Bible says that the earth is the Lord's and the fullness thereof and all that dwell therein.

God owns everything when you start to truly understand that you will never fall with God. I am not saying you won't have moments that it may look like you have fallen or failed but with God, you can get back up and try again. He will be with you and you will succeed or exceed your goal with God. You just have to trust Him in the process of what you are going through. He is with you and He is carrying you to the place called 'there.' 'There' is the destination where you are going if you don't give up.

Also, in some cases, you have to do it in fear, that is what I did multiple times. I am a full time entrepreneur and I have to depend on God for my finances, that can be very scary, but even though I feared initially leaving my job, I did it anyway, because God have a bigger plan for me and that is why He closed doors and opened them as well.

So when He closed the door to my job, there were so many doors that opened up that I could not do having a 9-5 job. So know that if God knows that He is opening a new door, it is much bigger than what you had before. God is in the business of the BIG; how do I know? Look at the stories in the Bible, what happened to Job when he lost everything he got double for his trouble. Look at David; he was a shepherd boy, and then later he became King with no kindred connection to the throne.

Look at Joseph; he went to almost dying in the pit to become second in command in the palace. So just like all of them that God blessed with the BIG. He is now ready to bless you with the BIG also. However, are you ready to flow with God and walk this journey with Him to see your blessed place? Walking with God does not mean it is going to be easy; it just gives you confidence that God is with you and you are not on this journey alone. If you do it His way, you are guaranteed success; you may ask how it would be guaranteed? The Bible says:

"This is the [remarkable degree of] confidence which we [as believers are entitled to] have before him: that if we ask according

to his will. [that is, consistent with his plan and purpose] he hears us." 1 John 5:14

So this verse explains to us that God only hears the prayers for only the will of God in our lives. It has to be subject to His will; you cannot want to desire something that is not according to God's plan when you are His child. People talk about permissive will, it is not valid. It is not biblically sound. If there was such thing as a permissive will, then why would we need God? It just doesn't make sense.

It is God's will or your own will. You have the choice of free will, but it does not mean God's blessing is on what you obtain. Meaning you got the wealth by lying about who you are. That is not the will of God. He wants you to get things the right way and through a process. Through Him by following His steps to get there so He can get the glory out of your life. Anything good can be the will of God, but you have to stay in prayer and ask Him if this is something that He wants you to do. God's will allow you to walk into purpose, and that is why He draws us closer to Him so we can see what He has for us.

Following God is more straightforward than doing it on your own. God gives you insight that you cannot get on your own. He shows you an easier path to get to your destination. That is why it is good to choose faith over fear because He is with you, so there is no need to fear anything. That is how you have faith over fear. Know that fear is an emotion that you can change when you believe the opposite of what you fear. Anything emotional can be changed; you just have to change your mind and thoughts. The Bible talks about it clear it says:

"Finally, believers, whatever is true, whatever is honorable and

worthy of respect, whatever is right and confirmed by God's word, whatever is pure and wholesome, whatever is lovely and brings peace, whatever is admirable and of good repute; if there is any excellence, if there is anything worthy of praise, think continually on these things [center your mind on them, and implant them in your heart]." Philippians 4:8

So when you think about the right things, fear is eliminated from your life like it never existed. If you choose faith over fear, then fear cannot overtake your mind and your thoughts. You will be a walking faith machine; you will always take faith, have faith and be faith. Faith will become a part of you; anytime that fear steps in, you will recognize it right away, because you have been walking in faith so long you know its heartbeat.

You will be able to tell the difference between faith and fear. I know this because that is what I walk in every day, I know the difference now, but at the beginning, I didn't because I walked in a lot of fear at one point so I could not tell. I used to speak words of doubt like "I can't do this," "I'm tired of this," "I don't think this will work," and so on. That is when fear will come upon you speaking like that. But as you grow in faith, you can definitely see the difference when you walk in either faith or fear.

When you walk in faith, you have to turn those words of doubt that you used to speak into words of faith; this will give you power over the enemy. For example, "I am going to make this work," "I can do anything I put my mind to," "I have it in me to succeed," "God has created a strong brilliant man or woman," etc.... This will help you to build your faith muscle when you do this daily. Speak these faith words over your life, and you will overcome fear every time. When you have thoughts of doubt, use your words of faith out loud to break those thoughts.

You don't have time to fear; you have so much work to do for the Lord. So whatever is going on in your life, deal with the root ask God to help you figure out what is stopping you and help you move forward into your future. God has more fantastic plans for you; you just have to know He does; He just wants you to believe He does. Don't doubt God; believe He loves you. He loves when His children believe in what He says, this makes God feel like He is doing a great job parenting us. He wants and knows that His children will succeed because we are in the right posture for Him to bless us. He loves to bless His children. God gets a joy out of doing so.

Chapter 15
Faith is Not Emotions

S ome people get baffled about what faith really is. Faith is not emotional; it is a mindset that you make a conscious decision to know that whatever you desire according to the will of God, you will have. Let's look at the definition of faith. It says that faith is complete trust or confidence in someone or something. So there is no emotion attached to that definition. That is why faith is not an emotion. Earlier in the book, we talked about different types of faith, but I only gave you one type, which is saving faith. I want to talk about the gift of faith. Faith is a gift given by God; the Bible says we all have a measure of faith. But we have the power to take our faith to another level.

Let's look at David in the Bible, for example; when he was a young boy, he had to take out a huge giant that could have knocked him out with one blow, but because he had this faith in God and also what God allowed him to do in the past which was to kill the lion and the bear. So by his past experience, God was telling him if I did that, then I can do this. He believed that he can take this giant out when everyone around him was afraid. He did not need any armor, just his slingshot and stones. He used his gift of faith on another level. Do you want to do that? Are you using your gift that God has given you to the max, or are you wasting time, making excuses, and getting caught up in your emotions?

Our flesh or we as humans do not want to do anything; we are naturally lazy people, not saying that we want to be lazy. But if we did not have to work to make money, most of us would not. Or we go by how we feel to do something, or we need some type of push to go after our dreams. I am just saying our emotions can take over if we are not careful. The Bible says this:

"Keep actively watching and praying that you may not come into temptation; the spirit is willing, but the body is weak." Matthew 26:41

So that is why we have to move by the Spirit of God. We may not want to do it, but God is telling us to do it for the new level He is about to take us. That is why we cannot obey our emotions. We have to obey the Spirit of God. For example, some of us have children, right? Do you feel like taking care of your children all the time? Most likely, your answer would be no; if you say yes, stop lying. All of us get worn-out and tired, but when we don't move in our emotions we will not jeopardize our future and legacy, it will be all worth it.

God wants us to get out of ourselves and what we want to do and do it His way, but to do it His way, we have to get out of our emotions. We are not always going to feel like doing something that God wants us to do. So we have to learn that we have power over our emotions. We tell our emotions what to do, not give into them.

A lot of the times, as people, we give in to our emotions, and then there is a consequence for what we did. We want to make excuses for the mishandling of our emotions to make ourselves feel better. Why do we do that? I think we do that because we want to present ourselves in front of people as perfect with no flaws, and everyone is flawed but you.

But clearly, everyone around us knows that we are imperfect, but we sometimes want to put up a facade and act like something we are not. We are just embarrassing ourselves and don't even know it. Everyone is just sitting there laughing at our foolery. If you believe it or not, we will never be perfect, and that is the truth.

We need to be real and make better choices in what we do, and when we mess up, we need to take responsibility like a grown-up. You will see that people will respect us more when you are honest and transparent. When we front, we are only fooling ourselves, not people. You have to give people credit. Most of them know you are fronting; they are just not going to tell you. So we have to be true to ourselves and have control of our emotions and our reactions.

We always have control over how we respond in every situation, some of us may say we don't, but we do. People have lost spouses, jobs, and friends and so on, because of negative reactions and emotions. You don't want to be the only one standing there with no one around you, because of how you behave. This is not the definition of faith, but this is showing you that faith has nothing to do with your emotions.

If we are not careful, our emotions can stagnate our faith. It can stop a door from opening for us through the most influential people that you may not have direct contact with them. But someone you know or meet will have that connection. So if you have a negative demeanor, people see that and may not want to deal with you. You don't know who can connect you to who.

This can be a destiny door, but because you cuss the door man out, they may know someone who can help you reach the next level in your career. You just closed the door right in your face and did not even know it. Faith is the opposite of your emotions. It is not the same. It contradicts each other. Faith is patient, and it waits; emotions are erratic and out of control if you let them and can be very harmful to someone else if used negatively.

Knowing that faith is beyond what you feel, it is not seen; it is only what you believe you will have. As I write these next words in this book, I know that I am going to be a millionaire and you may read this book at that time when I am walking in these very same words that I wrote. This book was written in the year 2020; I am putting the year so you understand that I am not there right now but will be.

Your words have so much power if you speak good or bad. So speak the right words, and you have to declare this over your life of what you want to see and believe it and start creating a plan towards what you want so you can get to the place where you first believed in your imagination.

Your dreams will never fall in your lap; you have to work to get what you want out of your own life, with God guiding you along the way. He will give you direction in what He wants you to do, and when you pray for God's will, it will become your desire as well as God's desires. Now you are in alignment for your blessings. He instructed me to write this book on faith so His people can truly understand what faith is all about. It is not just saying that you have faith. It is action behind it with strong patience.

You will get to your destined place when you allow faith to overpower your emotions. Decree over your life, what you want to see, and then ask God to give a blueprint of how to get there, and you will see your life change forever. That is how you get out of your emotions by trusting God.

Know that God's purpose and will for your life are more significant than you. That is why God pushes His people to go where He desires to take us. The reason why God pushes us is that He knows we have it in us to win, and He knows what it takes to get there. He has also placed inside of us the capacity to get the job done, we may not know it, but God does.

Sometimes we feel that we cannot take it anymore, but the Lord knows how much we can take. Did you ever experience a time when you were at your wit's end, and then strength comes upon you to finish what you started? That was the God that was within you that gave you the ability to finish, even when you thought you could not complete the task on your own.

That was your helper, the Holy Spirit stepping in to give you just enough strength to get it done. This strength only comes when you genuinely desire to do it, not when you don't want to do anything. God only helps those that really want the help, not someone that want the work done for them. When you truly desire to do something, God gives you the strength to do it, but he also gives you the power to decide if you will do it or not.

There are times that I feel worn-out, but I knew I had to get something done first. I make the decision in my mind to do it, then I take action to do it, and what does God do, He shows up, and somehow I feel His strength come upon me, and now I feel I can really do it now. That is what God does, but He needs us to decide.

God uses the Holy Spirit, which is our helper that Jesus left us when He died on the cross. He guides and leads us if we know how to use Him in our lives. Jesus said this in the Bible:

"But you will receive power and ability when the Holy Spirit comes upon you; and you will be My witnesses [to tell people about Me] both in Jerusalem and in all Judea, and Samaria, and even to the ends of the earth." Acts 1:8

So Jesus left us a part of Himself when He died, and that is the Holy Spirit. Many times we ignore the Holy Spirit; trust me, I have plenty of times and had to repent for it, but when I did recognize Him, then it was a supernatural strength that came upon me to finish any tasks that I had, and also He guided me through some issues that I was dealing with internally.

That is why the Holy Spirit is in a position to accomplish something I could not do. That is why we must trust God and not our emotions. That is why your faith is not emotions; it is believing and taking action toward your dreams and your goals that you set for your life. So this is very important to know about your emotions and faith that they are the opposite of each other they don't mix.

As people, we have to get a hold of our emotions and make better choices and decisions because if we don't, we will find ourselves in the same spot for 10 years and wonder where all that time went. The time went in being distracted for what we were supposed to be doing, which is walking in God's purpose and plan for our lives. By taking the necessary steps toward our destiny. I said this on Facebook a while back; I said that when God said to wait on Him, He meant work and wait. That is why some of the prophesies did not come to pass in your life.

This is so true because sometimes we think we are waiting for God to drop it out of the sky. Ouch, I know that hurts, but it is a true statement. We all want to hear the prophetic word, but we do not want to work that prophetic word out. That is called the in-between, the process, meaning it takes work to get where God said that you are going.

God has major plans for our lives, but we give up too easily, so we do not see the outcome because we don't want to wait to see what the end will look like. The end could be 10 years, or the end could be 6 months. We just have to ask God to give us the strength to endure. We will only see the outcome that we desire because it will take God and us to bring our future into fruition; what do I mean by that. If I did not write this book, it wouldn't have been published, and you would not be reading this right now.

My part is writing the book, and God's part is making sure that I have the funds to produce the book to get it in your hands; also, as I market the book, God will compel the people to purchase the book. You see how that works, it is not a poof, and everything is written and published. It took almost a year to write and publish this book. It would have taken a shorter time, but I stop writing for 4 months because I had no time or I did not take the time to write it. Then finally I decided to pick it up again and finished what I started. I say that to say this, you can pick up whatever you dropped. I don't care if it was 10 years; ago, you can be a finisher it does not matter when you finish it just matters that you do finish.

Some people start something and do not finish, you know God told me what that was, and I know this is going to sound funny because I use to battle with finishing anything. I had a slew of half-read books lying around. But to get back to what God said, He said that you have the spirit of incomplete. I was like, Lord, what is that? He said every time you started something, you never finished it. It could be anything. reading a book, working consistently in my business, drinking a bottle of water. I just had issues finishing anything.

This was stopping me in every area of my life and I did not want to hold myself back anymore. So I started to rebuke that spirit off of my life and declared and decreed that I would be a finisher. I prayed and prayed and made a decision that I was not going to live my life like that anymore. When I did, I started doing better; I started finishing books, finished writing my first book, and consistently ran my businesses. The only thing I still struggle with is finishing those bottles of water. I am not quite there yet.

I am determined to live a full, complete, and fulfilled life in Jesus Christ. I want to be one of the people in my family that they can look up to and be inspired by. To follow in my footsteps in a way to go after their dreams and to get all that God has for them. God has so much for His people, but the issue is that they fall into the trap of their emotions, thinking God will magically open the door because they are emotional; however, God is going to have empathy for them. Yes, God is gracious to us in our need, but God knows that we are capable people. If He did not, He would not have given us a brain and the right to choose. He might as well created robots if he was going to do that. But God did not want to build robots. He wanted us to stand on our two feet and fight for what is already ours.

That is why God said in His word to go and possess the land, meaning to take over by force, not violence, but strategically taking over based on His instructions on how to do it. This takes work on our part to make this happen. But God knows that we can do it, and His supernatural strength will empower us when we get weak and tired. He has strength waiting for us after we use all of ours. We have to show God that we are serious about His purpose and plan for our lives then He will start moving on our behalf.

When it comes to our emotions, it is okay to take a break; I am not saying to work yourself to death and not be emotional. I am saying that you don't always move in your emotions because you just don't feel like doing anything. Just know when you need a break, take that break and reset and start fresh. I would say every 90 days take a 2 to 3 day break to refresh and recharge. That is what I do to keep me centered and strong. That is healthy emotions, I just want you to know that you can do it, but make sure that you do not stop yourself from the most significant breakthrough or outcome in your life because you just want to stop and quit.

Chapter 16

Faith is a Step-by-Step Process

You have to view faith as step by step. New level, to new level. When you have faith in something, it does not all happen at one time. It all happens in steps. For example, you believe in God for a house and you don't have any money. But you move by faith anyway, and when you go through the steps to purchase your home, God starts to release funds either you did not know you had or someone blesses you with cash or anything that God will do to help you get that house. This actually has happened to me. That is why I mentioned this. I had to take steps and believe God that He would honor my faith and provide me the funding to get my first house, and He did, so that is what I mean, when you take steps to believe God for something, you will see the move of God.

You may ask the question, what if you don't hear God to move yet? Should you wait? This is my question: Is it a sin to move by faith in something or does God love when you believe Him for something. In the Bible it says:

"What is the benefit, my fellow believers, if someone claims to have faith but has no [good] works [as evidence]? Can that [kind

*of] faith save him? [No, a mere claim of faith is not sufficient—
genuine faith produces good works.]"* James 2:14

This scripture says that you must have faith connected to your
works; it is your evidence to God. It is also pleasing Him because,
in Hebrews, it says that it is impossible to please God without
faith. So in order to have true faith or genuine faith, like the Bible
says, it takes action on your part. Know if you move too quick,
God will still honor your faith and redirect you, but you still have
to just go for it anyway; even if you fail, that is all a part of this
faith walk.

Everything may not work out exactly how you want it, but God is
watching you and your faith, and it is just a matter of time things
will start to open up to the point that you will be overwhelmed
with God's blessings. God wants to bless His people
tremendously, but He needs something to work with to
supernaturally increase what is in your hand. That is why in
Deuteronomy, God said that He will bless the works of your
hands, not just your hands but the work of it.

So we got to get to work so God can take us to another place in
our lives and in our faith. Don't you know that the more you walk
in faith, the more confident you are in God? I know that for myself
to be true, because of all the things I walked through in life. I
know God will take care of me, but my job is to believe and work
the principle of faith, and that is working towards my dreams and
goals that God gave me, which is my business. I thank God that
He took me down this path of faith because it has truly
strengthened my faith, my mind and also have a standard in faith
that I will never give up no matter what it looks like and what I
have to face.

My faith is what keeps me focus and consistent and I know I will see days that will blow my mind. Don't you want to see that? Don't you want God to bless you supernaturally that it will blow your mind to a point it feels like you are dreaming. That has happened to me a few times, and don't you want that for yourself? The Bible says in Ephesians 3:20 it says,

"Now unto him that is able to do exceedingly and abundantly above what you can ask or think according to the power that worketh in us. Does that sounds like God wants to blow our minds or what."

It sure does sound like that to me. God is waiting on us to first believe, but there are steps to take to get there, don't overwhelm yourself with all the details just take one thing at a time. That is how you build your house from the ground up. Don't think it will happen all in one day because it will not.

Because if you believe that, then you will be disappointed and heartbroken and the devil or the enemy I should say, wants you to quit before you get there. That his plan is for you to never see the outcome of your work. If you don't plant a seed, then you will not have a harvest. It is important that you plant seeds then as your water it you will start to see growth. Growth is essential in the life period; in order for you to get more out of life you must grow internally to get more.

The things you had yesterday may not be enough to do for the things you have to do today or for your tomorrow to be successful. If you desire to be a millionaire, you have to have a millionaire mindset. How do you get that type of mindset? Read books that millionaires wrote to give you an idea of how millionaires think, do, and how they grow into million-dollar status.

I read books on successful people for my growth. I would recommend reading *Millionaire Success Habits* by Dean Graziosi, a book called *Go For No* by Richard Fenton & Andrea Waltz. These kinds of books will change your mind concerning your life and business and how you also think, read books of Empowerment as well. One book I read was *Brain Beauty* by Kim Lee King.

It was definitely speaking to women but the book was amazing. I loved every minute of reading it. It talks about makeup and how it can relate to your life and who you are, and who's you are. I would go on Amazon right now to purchase these jewels.

Just know that there is nowhere that you cannot go if God has given you access there. You have to know that with all of your heart that your faith is unlimited; there is no cap in God. He will take you places in your life that you would have never thought you would be in a million years. That is how the Lord works; you can be sitting somewhere with a dream that you are working on, and then BOOM, because all of your hard work doors start to fly open, and you in a place with so many options to choose from and you have to pray to the Lord which ones to take because it is so overwhelming.

That is how it all works when it comes to your faith. You believe, take action, meaning steps toward your goal, and then through time, watch God work on your behalf. Just know that your walk are steps, don't make it harder than it has to be. If you do you will get nothing accomplished and done. This book was written step by step, not in one day.

I have a writing schedule that allowed me to finish and complete what I started. So you have to know that this is how faith truly works in our lives. I think if we changed our perspective on faith, then more people will go after their dreams no matter what things may look like in front of them. They will just know with all of their hearts that God will do it for them no matter how long it takes for it to happen in their lives. Faith does not have a time limit; it happens in God's perfect time. As humans, we do not want to wait; we want instant gratification, that is not how faith works. That is not real faith; faith is when you believe something to happen in your life in the near future or future.

You can have faith in something for 20 years, and then it happens, does that mean it was not faith. Actually, to me, that was extreme faith because you believed in God for such a long time. Faith is a process that has to take its course, and what you believe for is ready to be released in your life; it will happen in time. Don't get mad because something does not happen right away.

Rejoice because everything you do to get where you want to be is getting one step closer every day. So keep on pushing and striving for the better, because better days lie ahead of you. I am not saying that it will not get frustrating at times, but what I am saying don't give up or stay angry because things don't work out like you have planned it.

This is how I resolve my frustration, so when I get frustrated, not very often but when I have a moment like we all do. I give myself 24 hours or less to get my bearings or my emotions right so I can still keep flowing in my productivity. I don't want to break the flow of my progress by moping for weeks on end, and then I am wondering why I don't see overflow.

So maybe this will work for you, if this does, do it because the world needs you to make it. There are so many people waiting for you to thrive and help them to be better like this book is doing right now. Well, I hope it is; if not, I don't know what to tell you at this point. The point is, WAKE UP!!! There is a world waiting for you to see your potential in who you are and how you can change the world for the better.

Also, be grateful for where you are today because you are not where you used to be. God sees and knows all. He knows what you are in need of before you ask for it. Isaiah 65:24 says

"It shall come to pass that before they call I will answer; and while they are speaking I will hear."

So God knows what you will ask for before you ask it, but you are still required to ask because of our own belief, not God. God wants us to ask and declare, so we believe God for what we are praying for. Also, God wants to know if this is truly what you want and can you believe him and take action in order to achieve what you believing him for.

Some things take prayer, and some things take action on our end. For example, you may be terminally ill, and you are praying to God for healing and a miracle. Then that is when prayer is required because you cannot heal a sick body.

But say you want a better job and you are praying for God to open the door for you. Then you have to make the necessary steps to fill out the application, prepare for an interview even if you got the job without it, or if you had to go through the interview process, God will touch the person's heart to hire you for that job.

You always have to prepare for everything, even when God favors you a different way. I will use myself, for example. God told me to partner up with a Real Estate Company to make money in my Real Estate business. Even though I knew someone who was a part of the company, I still prepared a proposal to make an agreement.

I did not really need it, but they were so impressed that I did all of that to get their attention because everything was approved before they read the proposal, but I still had to be ready because I may have needed the proposal to get approved. So what if I did not prepare, it would have shown God that I don't take my business seriously and I just wanted everything handed to me without work.

I believe God opened that door for me because I was professional in my approach. When you become a professional in faith God will bless you abundantly. This is very important when it comes to your faith. You have to show up to your blessing, being ready. This will allow God to give you favor with man. Remember, man, looks at the outer appearance God looks at the heart; you have to look a certain way to man for them to respect you.

But God wants you at your best anyway because you are representing Him. You don't want to represent God any kind of way; you would want to make Him proud. I know I do, so when you do things in excellence, you make God proud. He gives His people the best that is why we should look the best. We are Royalty just like 1st Peter 2:9

"But you are A CHOSEN RACE, A royal PRIESTHOOD, A CONSECRATED NATION, A [special] PEOPLE FOR God's OWN POSSESSION, so that you may proclaim the excellencies [the wonderful deeds and virtues and perfections] of Him who called you out of darkness into His marvelous light."

God, in a nutshell, told us who we are and how we should act. If we learn to take faith seriously and walk by it step by step, we can conquer any obstacle that tries to get in our way. We may stumble and fall, but what do we do? We get back up and try again.

I said this quote before. *"Don't let your failure be your Retirement"* in life, you will fail, but that just means you are getting closer to success because eventually you will run out of failures, and you will bump into success and have consistencies in it. If you walk by consistent faith, you will start to see constant success in your life, but if you stop and go, you will only experience sprinkles of success in your life and not the full potential of what is inside of you.

Sometimes when you fail at executing an idea, you have to make a small tweak, and then it may work out. You just keep on trying by being creative in what you are trying to accomplish.

My Coach Shalena said this, *'when you are going after your dreams, you are like a mad scientist because you are trying to figure out what works and what does not.'* So keep on trying and don't give up you will hit your target and succeed.

Chapter 17

Enjoy your Faith Journey

This chapter is very significant, and I did not realize it until I got to this chapter. 17 in the Bible means "Overcoming the enemy and Complete Victory" You have complete victory in your life. After reading 17 chapters, on faith, you should be prepared to defeat any obstacle that will try to choke the word that God has given you and the dream that is on the inside of your heart. I am so glad God allowed me to write this book to all of you reading this.

To be honest, they were days I was writing this book, and I was low in my spirit, but somehow when I was writing, it lifted me up, so I thank God for this book because it blessed me as much that I hope it blesses you.

I want to also thank you for taking the time to purchase and reading this book. Everything in this book was God-inspired and powerful and will be very important to your faith walk and journey. But this chapter is vital to your future success, because if you don't follow the steps in this chapter, you will fail to do anything else in this book because you will quit. So this is something that you should take with you at all times. Do you know what that is? Your JOY, do not ever lose that for your journey.

Joy is not from this world, but it is from God, and when you are His child, he can give you His joy. That is the reason that 'Enjoy' has the word joy in it. Joy is supposed to transform your mind in a space that it should be. It does not just come because you will always have circumstances and situations that are going on around you.

With Joy, it is the only certainty from God that everything will work out fine, so you don't need to stress out because God will work it out. You will have moments when you will have joy when you should be crying, but you are laughing. Does that make any sense to you? It probably doesn't because Joy is out from of this world.

Anything in life that does not make any sense, like being strong in a situation when you should be falling apart. That is not normal, so it has to be from God. When everything in your life is chaotic, and you have joy in your heart. Only God himself can do that. I mentioned God a lot because joy is supernatural. It just doesn't make sense. So when your life doesn't make sense, turn on the joy of the Lord, and to God, it makes sense to him to know what you require, and He is going to do everything in His power to work out what you are going through.

The Bible says in Nehemiah 8:10, *"The Joy of the Lord is My Strength"* so you know having joy in your life is essential because it gives you strength for your journey. So this is what you truly need along with your faith walk in God. Because there are times that things can go completely opposite in your life and you have to believe God for the turn around, but in the midst, God wants you to have peace and joy while you wait on Him to change your situation.

What I noticed in my walk when it came to my faith I was always up and down. I believed God sometimes, and then I got frustrated and impatient and doubtful because I allowed my flesh to get in the way of God's word and what he has promised me already.

So when you feel like this, this is not true faith; the Bible talks about faith clearly. In James 1:2-4 says:

"Consider it nothing but joy, my brothers and sisters, whenever you fall into various trials, be assured that the testing of your faith [through experience] produces endurance [leading to spiritual maturity and inner peace] and let endurance have its perfect result and do a thorough work, so that you may be perfect and completely developed [in your faith] lacking in nothing."

In a nutshell, faith takes patience, and as a result of us being patient, we will have the peace and joy that comes with that. Because now you are truly dependent on God and not yourself, which is limited, but God, we are unlimited. So if we know that, then we don't have anything to worry about but know that God has us in the palm of His hands. I had to believe in God for a lot of stuff in my life. I had to even believe Him to give me my mind back.

You can read in complete detail in my first book, "The Mind Regulator" But when I was going through mental illness, I did not know what to do at times, but God told me that He would deliver me, and He did keep that promise. Was I patient? No, I was not because I lacked faith back then. I did not believe God can deliver my mind. I thought that I would be like that forever, but once again, God proved me wrong. But I am glad that happened because it builds my faith in believing God for other things. That is why the trials you face are necessary for your journey. It builds you up for the next thing that you are about to encounter.

So that is why in my life, my faith is much stronger than it was before. So that is why you should rejoice in tribulation because you are coming out; it is just a season in your life, not a lifetime. When you view it that way, you will not get caught up in what is happening now. You will look toward your future, no matter what you face.

You will also be grateful because you will get double for your trouble and double for your shame, and all you have gone through was to build you and get you ready for the next level in your life. Because you are going to go through it, but you have a choice on how you go through it. Either you go through it in patience and peace or go through it in doubt, frustration, pain, heartache, sadness, and depression. You have a choice we all do. But it is said that in this time in my life, I choose peace and how I get peace is through trusting God and being patient for the promise. If God promised you something, then why stress yourself all the way until you get it. It is all a waste of time and energy.

Are you really believing God by doing this? I don't think so because faith is not supposed to be stressful; faith is peaceful. It is your evidence, so you don't have to see it in the natural to believe it will happen. You just need approval from God and that is yes and Amen. God is not in the business of stressing you out for the promise, but he does expect his children to trust in him and be patient for it.

Like your children, do you give them everything you will give them when they are not ready for it? No, they have to be old enough for some of the blessings you will provide them when you think they are ready to receive it. Also, they have to be well behaved to get what they want as well. The same thing happens, God is our father, and when He releases His blessings to His children. Sometimes we are not ready for the blessings that he has for us.

We have to wait and we cannot wait in an ungrateful manner. Because God will automatically know that we are not ready for it. So that is why we have to wait patiently and be grateful for what God has already done in our life. That is when we are ready for the next big thing that God has for us. So God has to get us ready for the blessings that are coming for us by allowing us to wait to build our faith.

So we have to enjoy this process of life; it is the only way to our destiny that will allow us to be a peace when we get there. You don't want to get there miserable because no one wants to be around you, and you will not be able to stay where you are positioned. God also has us wait to get our posture right to keep the position that he opened up for us. Again, you will miss out on opportunities if you are not stable in our emotions and how you interact with people.

That is another reason God has us to wait. He is stabilizing our behavior of when we get there, we will not mess things up. So you have to have a good demeanor, your demeanor is everything when it comes to doing business, friendships, marriage, etc. Your attitude can make or break a situation. So you have to be very careful on what you do and how you act. That is how you truly walk in Unlimited Faith.

But the first step to walking in the Unlimited Is giving your heart to Jesus Christ and I want to help you do that.

So repeat this prayer after me and say this out loud;

"Lord Jesus, I am a sinner, and I believe you died and rose and you are coming back again, forgive me for all my sins and unrighteousness. Come into my heart, and I want to live for you and thank you for saving me."

Now you have complete access to the supernatural that God wanted to always give you. He is now ready to take you where you have never been before. ARE YOU READY?

In Conclusion

I Just wanted you to know that you should enjoy this journey that you decide with God to take in your life, because you want to walk in abundance consistently, not just sometimes, but all the time. Having unlimited faith takes building, and it is not overnight, but it is possible for you. So never get in a place of giving up.

God loves you, and He will see you through every situation, and you will see yourself on the other side that you were stressing about for no reason. Know that it is not easy, but it will be all worth it. I hope that you enjoyed reading this book as much as I enjoyed writing it. Keep the faith, and you will start to walk in the UNLIMITED!!!

ABOUT THE AUTHOR

Shakeema S. Perry was born on January 17, 1981, in Brooklyn, New York. She is a businesswoman and the owner of three companies. The first is Glee Bargain Centers (www.gleebargaincenters.com) that sales her books, inspirational t-shirts and other accessories. Her goal is to inspire many to be the best you and look good doing it. Her second company is Impact Realty Solutions (www.impactrealtysol.com) where she does wholesaling and partnerships with Real Estate Investors to help families to sale their homes quickly. Her third company is Purpose To Promise Academy (www.purposetopromise.com) where she is a Purpose & Business Coach that teaches her skillset in business and help woman to find their purpose and start, grow and maintain their businesses.

She also loves her family, her friends, and to travel. She is a very resilient Christian woman. She is pleasant and devoted, and she takes her faith very seriously. She advocates for what is right and how people and the ones who are close to her are treated. She was led by God to write this book and to share how faith works and how vital it is concerning your future.

She also wants you to know that life is not always easy, but you can overcome any obstacle that comes your way. First you have to have faith and believe in it and have God in your life to help you through it. You will see that it will all work out in the end. So she hopes that this book will impact your life to another level of faith. Unlimited faith that is, and help you to have a greater relationship with God. She wants you to know how real God is and he can do anything but fail. He is a God that loves and cares for his people and he wants us to succeed at the highest level and to give him all the glory that he deserves. So if you ready for this powerful faith book get ready for some nuggets that will change your life forever.

Made in the USA
Middletown, DE
19 March 2021